EAST CLIFTON AVENUE

A FAMILY TRILOGY *Book Two*

LA PROSIMMA GENERAZIONE – THE NEXT GENERATION

Frank Plateroti, EdD

Dedication

To all the generations of people and families whose love and courage gave them the fortitude to leave their homeland and family and settle in a new land so their children would have opportunities to create fulfilling and happy lives for themselves and their families.

Most of all, to those family members who stay together, and selflessly take care of the parents or other family members regardless of the self-sacrifice, situation, and challenges.

Author Notes

My name is Frank Plateroti. As in Book 1, I am not only the author but also what you would call the narrator. This is my story of the people and families who lived, loved, and died on East Clifton Avenue.

In Book One we are introduced to the Buonofortes who emigrated from Mussomeli, Sicily to Little Italy in lower Manhattan, to East Clifton Avenue in New Jersey. I shared the early chapters of my life growing up with my mother's family, which had a great impact on my life. It includes my grandmother's life stories, the "whispered family conversations," and the events I was part of and witnessed.

As in Book One, to tell the story of East Clifton Avenue, I needed to create a *non-fictional* and *fictional* framework and I then interspersed the true events, which took place in Sicily, Little Italy, New York, and Clifton, New Jersey. Some characters are real, while some are fictitious, which is necessary to connect the true stories. Otherwise, these stories would just be standalone, disjointed fragments without appreciating the full personalities of the characters involved. For that reason, I am guiding you through the story of East Clifton Avenue through the *fictitious* Buonoforte family with me as the grandson, Dean Fonte, the narrator. Although some of the characters may be similar to the actual "real-life" people, in no way is my intention to besmirch or villainize anyone. These are my memories and perceptions of events and the people involved.

Also, interwoven in the story, as in Book One, are life lessons that can be learned by not only the good things but the not-so-good things that, perhaps if one is keen-sighted, can be avoided. There are many underlying questions I wondered about growing up and observing life around me.

For example, what do we have to offer future generations? Why do bad family behaviors repeat themselves? How do we not make the same mistakes past generations have made in the name of "blood"?

With the story of East Clifton Avenue and the Buonfortes, perhaps some of those situations can be avoided.

Recap of Book One

On a cold and snowy end of January morning, Enzo Buonoforte leaves his house on East Clifton Avenue to clean the snow off his car so he can visit his son Donny. As Enzo looks around, he reminisces about his life and the people, past and present, who live in the neighborhood of East Clifton Avenue. Although it is after the Christmas holidays, with the snow falling, Enzo recalls his favorite time of year with his family, especially with his late son Pietro. Enzo also recalls that for some, East Clifton Avenue was their "street of dreams." Sadly, for others, their lives weren't as fortunate as the Buonofortes. Even so, for the Buonofortes, life was a challenge.

As Enzo removes the snow from his car, he suffers a heart attack. Through his dying, we see Enzo's childhood and experiences with his bitter and evil stepmother and his loving two stepsisters. We see a young boy who dramatically turns into a young man, becomes independent, and marries the love of his life, Anna Arnone. We follow Enzo's and Anna's lives from Mussomeli, Sicily, to Little Italy in Lower Manhattan, to finally settling with their eight children on East Clifton Avenue.

With Enzo's death, we witness the family aftermath as the result of what happens when one spouse dies and now leaves the other, who was so dependent on the one who passed away. We also witness the drama that ensues with the Buonoforte family, when it comes to the questions of: How do we take care of this parent now when we have our own family and respective spouses to take care of? Who will take the unwanted lead, and who will unfairly stand by, considering the situation just an unwanted burden? With Enzo's death, Anna is left with a future that is in serious doubt.

A flash forward reveals that Anna's immediate future has her living with her seventh child, Chiara, Chiara's husband Joseph, and their three sons, staying with the oldest son, Dean, in his bedroom. Although each of the other six Buonoforte children takes turns bringing Anna to their homes on Sundays, it still proves to be a challenge and restricts the time for Chiara and Joseph. When Anna's health deteriorates, it's decided at a contentious meeting with the seven Buonoforte children, that now that Anna needs constant care, there seems to be no choice but to place her in a nursing home. To the benefit of some and the dismay of others, it is decided to sell the Buonoforte home to pay the nursing home expenses. Often, the death of a loved one brings out the best and the worst in families. For the Buonofortes, unfortunately, it is the same situation.

Through flashbacks, we witness how close friends and relatives such as Don Carlo Masseria, Bruno Sessino, Howard Johnson, Enzo's stepsister Francesca, and others, dramatically crisscross and impact Enzo's and Anna's lives and their future.

Two mysteries are interwoven throughout the story, one is resolved in Book One; the other is carried over in Book Two. The first mystery is the relationship of the Buonoforte family to the head of the Paramus Nursing Home, who turns out to be Anna Buonoforte's long-lost goddaughter, Anna Avero. This is a fortunate discovery since the connection means a place for Anna in the nursing home, rather than on a waiting list. The second mystery concerns the original source and history of a crucifix under glass that belonged to Enzo's father in Sicily, which is now in the hands of Chiara and her husband Joseph.

With the preparation of Enzo's funeral and wake, family drama ensues as Anna Buonoforte uncharacteristically and angrily takes charge of the planning away from her son Jack, and makes the plans herself with the help of her daughter Chiara.

As the first afternoon of Enzo's wake begins and throughout the day, there is the usual drama related to the death of a loved one. Of course, Anna is especially heartbroken, as are the Buonoforte children, since Enzo's death is now a reality.

Book One ends with a mysterious guest arriving at the wake, whose identity is not revealed until here, in Book Two.

Main Characters

<u>The Buonoforte Family</u>

Enzo Buonoforte The main protagonist in the story and the Buonoforte patriarch and unelected "Mayor" of East Clifton Avenue. He is warm, affectionate, and clever. Devoted family man. When provoked, he can have a temper.

Anna Buonoforte Enzo's wife and the family matriarch. She can be aloof but is affectionate and caring. She is the mother of eight children and godmother to Anna Avero.

Maria Buonoforte Lerino First daughter of Enzo and Anna. She can be cold and unaffectionate.

Antonino Lerino Maria Buonoforte's husband. A hard worker and more affectionate than his wife.

Giusepina Buonoforte Litto Second daughter of Enzo and Anna. She is warm and affectionate, the exact opposite of Maria.

Pietro Buonoforte First son of Enzo and Anna. Just like Giusepina, he is warm and affectionate. A family favorite, especially to his sister Chiara. He is in an arranged marriage. His untimely death at thirty-five leaves his wife with three young children that the Buonofortes help take care of, especially Chiara. His death shakes the family to its core and changes the family dynamic.

Francesco Buonoforte The second son of Enzo and Anna. He is serious and aloof and is sometimes mistaken for a Hollywood actor. A favorite of Dean's.

Rita Buonoforte Petteri The third daughter of Enzo and Anna. She became responsible for the younger children, especially Chiara. She is somewhat overweight, self-centered, and secretly resentful of Chiara, but can be warm and affectionate.

Dante Petteri Husband of Rita. Originally from Northern Italy. A very good cook. He is handsome and "continental." Likes to try to "live large."

Giacomo "Jack" Buonoforte The third son of Enzo and Anna. He is handsome and charming with an athletic build. Arrogant and narcissistic. He is Chiara's nemesis.

Margo Buonoforte Wife of Jack Buonoforte. She is glamorous and cunning. Disappointed in the direction her life has gone and is bitter. Can be warm to those whom she chooses. She likes to imbibe.

Chiara Buonoforte-Fonte The fourth daughter of Enzo and Anna. She is slim, stunning, and the most attractive of the Buonoforte daughters. Like her father, she is clever and loves unconditionally, especially her three sons and her husband. She is very social and devoted to her Buonoforte family. Mother of three boys, with Dean Fonte being the oldest. She is also "high-strung" due to the death of her brother Pietro, with whom she was very close.

Joseph Fonte Husband of Chiara. Warm, caring, and very handsome, with jet-black hair and deep blue eyes. Like his wife, he loves unconditionally, especially his three sons. He is devoted to his wife. When provoked, he has a temper.

Dean Fonte Chiara's son and narrator of the story. He witnessed the many events of the Buonofortes and knows the family's stories and secrets, mostly from the stories told to him while taking care of his grandmother. Very much like his mother and grandfather.

Donatello "Donny" Buonoforte The youngest child of Enzo and Anna. He has a place in everyone's heart. Very close to his parents.

Giuseppe Buonoforte Enzo's father. A widower who was forced to marry Julia, Enzo's stepmother. He is aloof and disappointed with his life and with the death of his first wife, Giulietta, Enzo's mother.

Julia Scarpa Buonoforte Enzo's stepmother—the proverbial evil stepmother who abuses Enzo and was made a widow from her first husband by a Mafia vendetta.

Rosalia Scarpa Julia's daughter and Enzo's stepsister. Opposite to her mother, she is warm and loves Enzo.

Francesca Scarpa Julia's second daughter and Enzo's stepsister. Like her sister Rosalia, she is warm and loves Enzo.

The Buonoforte Friends and Acquaintances

Tomasso Fassino aka "Old man Fassino" The Fassionos and the Buonofortes are close family friends since the Buonofortes moved on East Clifton Avenue.

Rabbi Merlino Enzo's teacher and mentor. A warm and affectionate man of God. A father figure.

Aunt Josephine Enzo's aunt on his mother's side. She is warm, affectionate, and considers Enzo her son after Enzo's mother dies. She leaves Enzo a small inheritance.

Antonino Scarpa Warm and caring. Uncle of Rosalia and Francesca who takes the two girls to live with him and his business partner Victor Roselli in Agrigento, Sicily.

Victor Rosselli A big, brawny man with a big heart to match. Antonino's business partner. Antonino found him in a street outside a bar where he was beaten and robbed. Antonino saved his life.

Angelina Maria Cesare A stunning, retired famous opera singer and restaurant owner who becomes Don Carlo's lover and mother of their daughter, Lucia.

Beatrice Ceasare Sister of Angelina and wife of Carlo Masseria after the passing of Angelina Maria Cesare

Carlo Masseria Also known as Don Carlo; runs a numbers racket because of his uncanny ability to calculate numbers and betting odds. He has a photographic memory. Lover of Angelina Cesare. With the changing times, Carlo invests in legitimate businesses and becomes a multi-millionaire.

Bruno Sessino Close friend of Carlo Masseria and Enzo Buonoforte.

Howard Johnson Also a close friend of Enzo Buonoforte and Carlo Masseria. A "colored man" who overcame bigoted obstacles, with the help of Carlo Masseria and Enzo.

Anna Avero Head of the Paramus nursing home with a secret that will dramatically affect all those around her, including the Buonofortes.

Stefano San Giorgio Birthfather of Anna Avero. Father of Anna's half-brothers, Morris and Luca, and half-sister, Loretta.

Father Ludovico (Gianni Rudolfo Genco Russo) Catholic priest from Rome and eventually assistant pastor at Sacred Heart Church in Clifton, New Jersey.

Father Tommaso (Tommaso di Caltanisetta) A close friend and mentor to Father Ludovico.

Chapter 1
Enzo Buonoforte's Wake, January 28, 1963

Chiara, Joseph, and Anna got to the funeral home earlier than the two o'clock viewing to go over the funeral arrangements and car placement for when they drive to the cemetery. When they pulled into the parking lot, except for the funeral director's car and the hearse, the parking lot was empty. Joseph helped Anna get out of the car, and when they got inside, the first thing they saw was the directory with Enzo's name, directing people to the east viewing room. When Chiara and Anna saw Enzo's name, it was at that point they knew his death was a reality; he was gone. Just the simple directory with Enzo's name made it real.

Joseph didn't let Anna or Chiara linger at the directory and walked them to the funeral director's office. Joseph ushered Anna to a chair inside the office. They talked with the funeral director and went over all the final arrangements. They also paid the balance for the wake and the funeral. It was just one more thing they wouldn't have to worry about or have to return to do after the funeral. The funeral director shook both Chiara's and Joseph's hands, offered his condolences in Italian to Anna, and helped her out of her chair.

As they left the office, he said, "We would again like to offer our condolences, and both my son and I will be with you to take care of everything. Father Ludovico will be here in the evening to say prayers before the wake is over. Would you like to see your father at this time?"

Chiara thought it was such an odd question. It was as if he were a piece of art or a piece of furniture that was being unveiled.

"Thank you, but I will wait for the rest of my family. And thank you again for everything you have done," Chiara replied.

Then Joseph quietly whispered to Chiara, "Maybe you should go in and make sure everything looks okay."

Chiara just shook her head. "No, I want to wait."

Joseph could see her eyes were teary, and he didn't say anything else.

Around twenty minutes later, almost all of Anna's children arrived with their spouses and a few with the older grandchildren. Some people went down to the restroom area where there was also a smoking room. It wasn't long before the smell of smoke wafted upstairs along with the talking that was getting louder. It was annoying Chiara, who asked Joseph to go downstairs and tell the people to keep the noise down. They could also hear Margo's loud voice as she was giving Jack instructions to help her get her coat off. The funeral director even looked where he heard someone "shushing" Margo.

Anna, Chiara, and Joseph were escorted to the glass French doors of the viewing room, where the family somberly greeted each other as they arrived, making sure they first greeted and kissed Anna. The newly arrived people began coming from downstairs and waited behind the Buonoforte family. The doors to the viewing room were covered with lace curtains, and through the blur of the curtains, you could see the flowers lining the walls on either side of the coffin. There were touché lamps on each side of the coffin with pink light bulbs that placed a soft glow on the coffin and Enzo's face. The coffin was closed halfway, so you could only see Enzo's upper torso. Because he didn't suffer through an illness, he looked as if he was just sleeping, although he looked small in the coffin.

As Chiara was standing in front of the doors, she realized she couldn't remember if it was the same as her brother Pietro's wake. *Did I just block it out of my mind?* she thought. Her thoughts were suddenly interrupted when she saw the funeral director coming from the doorway inside of the viewing room. He looked at the coffin for a second and then walked toward the glass doors to open them for the family. As he came closer, there were a few moments of silence and nervous anticipation and then began the sound of crying. Turning around, Chiara saw it was her sisters, and Chiara tried not to get emotional. She gave them a look to stop, motioning to their mother. She was holding Anna's arm on one side, with Joseph on the other. Then suddenly Anna wobbled as if she was going to fall.

"Momma!"

Joseph could help Anna on his side of her, but she was too heavy for Chiara. Maria and Rita screamed, but they just stood where they were. Jack scrambled to help Chiara as Anna started to fall backward. Jack and Joseph caught her and helped her stand. Chiara could see the funeral director coming toward the door and waved to him not to open the doors. He understood and instead of opening the glass doors; he ran to the side door of the viewing room and came into the waiting area to assist. Joseph and Jack helped Anna to a nearby couch and the funeral director came over with a paper cup of water. Anna took a few sips and then waved it away.

"Look at what your father is doing to me. Even when he's dead, he..." She broke down and cried. Chiara sat next to her and held her hand.

"It's ok, Momma."

"No. It's not ok. I always thought we would die at the same time. I don't know why, but I just did. Who am I going to talk to? Who knows me? What am I going to do without him except maybe be a burden? I can't live by myself and I don't want to go into an old age home."

"Momma, don't worry. We'll take care of you. I promise. You'll be fine. Don't worry. I promise."

Anna took Chiara's face in her two hands and kissed her.

"I know. Ti amo bella."

Rita walked over and motioned for Chiara to come to the side with her. Chiara got up and Maria took her place next to Anna and held Anna's hands. Chiara was a little annoyed that Rita wanted to see her at this specific time. *What could be that important?* she thought. "What do you want?" she asked.

"I didn't want to tell you before in front of Momma, but I think I should tell you. I just talked to Don Carlo's daughter. She called the funeral home. I think he died last night."

"What do you mean, you *think* he died?"

"Well, Howard had called Don Carlo and confirmed with Don Carlo's daughter the time of the wake and funeral arrangements. Then, when his daughter called back here and the funeral director saw you were busy with Momma, I spoke to her. She said she went into the den carrying a tray with the expresso and a few cookies. It looked as if her father was sleeping. She called to her father. His head was to the side and his mouth was open. She went to place the tray down, but when she saw his face, she realized he wasn't sleeping. The glasses that were dangling from his hand dropped to the ground. She missed the coffee table and everything crashed to the floor. There were a lot of people nearby when I was talking to her and there was a lot of noise and it sounded like she was crying. She said something about the funeral home and the other line on the phone rang and I told her I would call her back and I hung up."

"I don't have time for this now. Jesus. Don't tell Momma anything."

Rita stood silently. Joseph signaled for Chiara to come to him because Anna wanted to get up and go to the viewing room.

"Ok. Tell me later. It looks like Momma is getting up to go in."

Rita walked in front of Chiara and pointed toward the stairway entrance.

"Chiara, look who just came in."

Chiara turned to look past the people walking up the stairs from the entrance. "Jesus," Chiara said, "what the hell is he doing here? How did he get here?"

Joseph walked over to see their son, Dean, who was wearing a suit a little too small for him.

"Hey, Dad."

Joseph pulled Dean by his jacket collar to the side where Chiara was standing and tried to whisper. "Don't 'hi dad' me. Who told you you could come here and how did you get here *and* who is watching your brothers?"

"I wanted to come. He's my grandfather too."

Chiara knew he was right and tried not to show that she was getting upset.

"How did you get here?" Chiara asked.

"Easy, Mom. I asked Junior to take me. He's trying to find a parking space. I told him you called, and you told me to ask him to take me and have Rietta watch the boys."

Junior, Rietta, and their son Robbie have lived next to Chiara and Joseph since they first moved to East Paterson. Joseph looked at Chiara and gently put his hand on Dean's shoulder.

"Go over there and sit and don't move. You're in enough trouble."

"I'm going to see Grandma first."

Joseph shrugged his shoulders and looked at Chiara, who shook her head.

"What can we do: he's right," Chiara said.

Dean kissed his grandmother and sat next to her. Dean's godmother, Janine, saw Dean, sat next to him, and put her arm around his shoulder.

"Hi, honey. Are you ok?"

Dean nodded.

"Dean, do you want me to take you in to see Grandpa?"

"I'll think I wanna wait."

"I understand. You know when somebody dies, I always try to remember a happy memory of them when they were alive. What is a happy memory you have of you and your grandfather?"

Dean thought for a few seconds. "When I was younger, he took me to the feast, just him and me. He let me go on the Ferris wheel and then we went into the church basement and we met some of his friends and they were really nice. They each gave me a quarter and wanted to buy me lunch there. But it was that tripe stuff, so I just said I wasn't hungry. Grandpa had bought me a sausage sandwich already, anyway. I couldn't finish it, so Grandpa did. They asked Grandpa if he wanted to play cards and he said he was going to take me to listen to the music and take me back to his house. I wanted to buy this little teddy bear on a stick, but I didn't have enough money. He told me to keep my money, and he bought it for me. I still have it. We listened to the band and the lady singer and I sat on the stairs and watched her the whole time. Then after, he talked to the lady who sang, and she was very nice. Grandpa was talking about her a few weeks ago cause now she is very famous. We went back to his house, and it was a great time. I will always remember that."

Janine had tears in her eyes. "See. That's a great story. Always remember that."

Joseph and Chiara wanted to help Anna get up to walk her to the viewing room, but Anna said she wanted to wait a few more minutes. Chiara whispered to Rita, who was standing on the side of Joseph.

"Did you hear anything more about Don Carlo?"

"I called again, but no one answered."

Chara just shook her head. "Rita, what exactly did his daughter say?"

"I remember her saying something about a funeral home but there were a lot of people talking in the background and she kept apologizing about not coming to the funeral..."

"But you said he *died*. How could you not get that straight?!" Chiara didn't want to show how angry she was and didn't want to make a scene in front of her mother.

"What's the difference..."

"What do you mean, what's the difference? If he's dead, it makes a big difference. You never get anything straight. Jesus."

Anna heard the whispering. "Che?"

"Nothing, Ma. We're trying to find out if Don Carlo is coming this afternoon or tonight," said Chiara.

Anna remained silent. Rita didn't say a word because she felt foolish not knowing if she got the message right. She was trying to go over it in her mind and didn't want to hear anything more from Chiara.

Anna was complaining about her knees. Chiara rubbed her mother's knees. She could see Anna's knees were getting worse and wondered how she would live alone.

Joseph walked over to the picture window and saw all the cars lining up. A police car pulled up and parked, and the officer got out of the car to direct traffic. Joseph went back to Chiara and Rita, shaking his head. "There are a lot of cars lined up to pull into the parking lot. There's a cop now directing traffic."

Chiara shook her head. "This place is going to be a madhouse."

"You're right. I think one car is the Violas. Do they have a green Buick?"

"How should I know?" Chiara shook her head, not really caring if it was the Violas or not.

The funeral director opened the French doors, letting out a rush of pungent aroma from flowers that are typically associated with funerals, and it was nauseating. Flowers lined both sides of the coffin and down both walls of the viewing room. Only the immediate family were allowed in the room so they could settle in before letting the people who were waiting behind the family and inside the vestibule.

The funeral director's assistant kept coming to the funeral director, saying that people were complaining because they had to wait in a line outside and it was freezing cold. The funeral director whispered to his assistant, "Open the other room and let people stand in there."

"Yes, but we're getting the room ready for that soldier."

"My God. I forgot about that. Did that guy from Washington call anymore?"

"Yes. He left a message for you to call ASAP to confirm the body's arrival and other stuff," said the assistant.

"Alright. As soon as I get the Buonoforte family settled in, I will call him back. I also have to talk to the Buonofortes because this may be a zoo tomorrow with all the reporters and...Oh, God."

Joseph and Chiara helped Anna to her feet, and they walked into the viewing room toward the coffin. As Anna approached the coffin, she stopped. At first, she couldn't make out the person who was in the coffin because he looked so small. As she got closer, she could see it was Enzo, and she sobbed. Rita, Maria, and Giusepina followed and were all also sobbing. Chiara and Joseph focused on getting her mother to the coffin. Chiara was calm until she got closer to the coffin. Anna screamed in unintelligible Italian. Francesco and his wife followed them in. Margo and Jack were just coming through the door when Margo pulled at Jack's jacket so she could whisper in his ear.

"Let's wait. Oh, God, your mother is so hysterical and..."

They had already been arguing in the car and Jack had not had time to cool down and, combined with the anxiety of his father's wake, he lost his temper and grabbed onto Margo's arm. He pulled her out of the doorway, past the people in the back of them. He pulled her so hard that Margo almost lost one of her high heels. They quickly moved past everyone, not making eye contact, almost sprinting down the hallway toward the back of the funeral home.

"Jack, what the hell do you think you're doing?"

"Shut... the hell...up."

Jack looked around and saw a sign on a door with the word *Storage*. He opened it and saw a bunch of chairs piled on top of one another. He closed the door, took a chair from the pile, and told Margo to sit down, but she resisted him.

"I am not staying in here with you. You're an animal."

She reached for the doorknob and Jack grabbed her arm, pushed her in the chair, and leaned over her. "Don't you have any decency? My mother just lost the man she was married to for over fifty years. *For over fifty years!* How do you expect her to act?"

Margo could see such rage in Jack's eyes. She couldn't remember the last time she saw him so angry. She always knew when to pull back, but this time she made the situation worse.

"You Sicilians and your mothers, you make me sick."

Jack raised his hand to hit her, but it was only a gesture. He would never hit a woman.

"Go ahead, Jack, hit me. You don't have the balls."

Jack dropped his arm but went after her again. "My mother was right. The only thing you care about is yourself and your own fucking family."

Margo knew now she had to back down. Weirdly, it excited her, but then that feeling passed. All Margo could think of was that Jack had already made a scene. What would people think? Jack silently looked straight at her for a couple of seconds. Neither one broke their stare; then Jack took a chair, put it right in front of her, and sat down.

"Do you love me? Did you ever love me? Do you love the kids at least?" he asked.

"I feel the way I always felt about you. And my God, of course, a mother loves her children!"

"YES, 'a mother.' I am talking about you!"

Once again, they stared at each other. There was a soft knock at the door before she could answer him. They were both startled. Before she could even make a move, Jack got up, moved his chair, gestured to her, and whispered. "Stay seated and shut up."

Jack slowly opened the door; it was the funeral director.

"Is everything alright? I saw you come in here and thought maybe your wife needed some assistance."

"Oh, thank you. My wife is very close to my family and when she saw my father in the coffin and how upset my mother was, she just felt faint.

Jack looked over at Margo. "Isn't that right, *dear*?"

Margo gave a small nod and a smile.

"She is better now. We will be right out."

"Ok, Mr. Buonoforte. You can use my office."

"That's ok. We're fine here."

"If there is anything you need, please just ask."

"Thank you very much."

The undertaker left and Jack closed the door.

"Jack, you're gonna be sorry for this."

"I am already sorry. I've been sorry for years. Now, what you're gonna do is get up and when you go into the viewing room, you're gonna go over to my mother and offer your condolences."

"I'm going to the ladies' room first."

"My ass, you're gonna. You do what I say or your bags are going to be packed and you can move in with your family. And if you think I'm kidding, just fucking try me."

Jack went to help Margo stand, and she shunned his help. Jack opened the door and took her arm, and they walked over to the viewing room. They spotted where Dean was sitting on the couch outside the room.

Jack gave a disgusted stare and whispered under his breath, "*What the hell is he doing here?"*

Jack never liked Dean. Maybe it was because Dean was close to Anna and Enzo. Then again, he was Chiara's son, so perhaps that was another reason. He also felt that he should have made his two sons come. How is this going to look?

Margo started to walk over to Dean.

"Where are you going?"

"I want to see if Dean is ok."

Margo always liked Dean and Dean was very fond of Margo. With Margo, if she liked you, she was kind and generous. If she didn't, she was just cordial. Chiara and Joseph never discussed their feelings about Margo or any family member or family friends with their kids, so Dean could make his mind up about Margo and everyone else. For him, it was simple. If someone was nice to him, he was respectful and nice back. When Dean heard the whispers about Jack and Margo, he tried to ignore them.

"Hi, Dean. Are you ok, honey?"

"Hi, Aunt Margo. Yeah..."

Jack cut in. "How did you get here?"

Chiara heard Jack questioning Dean and walked over, put her hand on Dean's head, stroked his hair, and answered Jack before Dean had the chance.

"I asked Junior to bring him. We knew how much Dean wanted to pay his last respects to his grandfather, so on the way over here we decided to let him come and we called Junior. When are your kids coming?"

No answer.

Margo thought to herself, *Brava, Chiara!*

Dean was not surprised his mother stuck up for him. Chiara would protect her children at any cost; even with her own life. This was just a small gesture. Sicilians would kill for their children without a second thought.

Jack sneered and started walking away. Margo caressed Dean's chin with her hand and gave him a hug and a kiss on his cheek, smiled, and caught up to Jack, who had already walked toward the viewing room.

Suddenly Jack became very anxious because the reality that his father was lying in the coffin affected him and he began to tear up. Margo could see he was getting emotional but ignored it and just took his arm as a small gesture of support. Jack could see Anna standing at the side of the coffin talking to Enzo, which was such a sad sight that he began to cry. Margo went into her purse and offered her hankie to Jack, who waved it away and wiped his face with his hand. Even so, she held onto Jack's arm as they just waited to get to the coffin.

Anna was being consoled by so many people. Finally, Chiara and Joseph tried to guide Anna closer to the side of the coffin and away from what was becoming a small crowd of mourners. Joseph and Chiara were trying to move Anna to the kneeler and past the small group of mourners, who were crying and moaning in different undistinguishable Italian dialects. When the small group saw Anna was trying to get closer to the coffin, they began to disperse and find seats. Finally, Chiara and Joseph could help Anna to the gaudy gold kneeler. It had a red velvet pad to kneel on and a red velvet arm cushion supported by four golden angels. But instead of kneeling, Anna suddenly reached over the side of the coffin and started screaming, grabbing Enzo's arm as if to try to wake him. The whole coffin shook and the flower blanket on top of the coffin almost fell off; rescued by Joseph. Onlookers gasped at such a pitiful sight while Joseph tried to gently restrain her.

The funeral director, seeing what was going on, gasped and practically sprinted to gently help Chiara calm Anna and have her kneel, taking her hands off Enzo's arm. Once again, there was a sudden outburst of crying and screaming as onlookers could see what was happening. Standing over her mother to calm her down, Chiara's tears fell on Anna's head, with Anna looking up. There was a thin line between tragedy and comedy with what was happening. Chiara almost laughed.

Seeing that Joseph and Chiara were holding Anna's arms, the funeral director stepped back, took a handkerchief from his jacket pocket, wiped his forehead, and breathed a sense of relief. He walked slowly backward to make room for the other Buonoforte children, who were waiting to get to the coffin.

With Anna in position on the kneeler, everyone suddenly quieted down. Joseph stepped back to let the rest of the family get closer to Anna. Chiara kneeled next to Anna while her other sons, daughters, and their spouses stood behind Anna. This moment of silence was shattered when Anna reached over again, trying to shake Enzo's arm, screaming for him to wake up. Chiara gently took Anna's arm away and there was another wave of tears and sobs.

"Momma, please. Poppa wouldn't want to see you like this. Come now and sit down and give everyone else a chance."

Joseph, seeing that no one was going to move out of his way, quietly excused himself and helped Chiara lift Anna off the kneeler pulling her arm back. With their help, Anna got up to give the others a chance to kneel next to the coffin.

Chiara was sobbing but tried to calm down to focus on her mother. Again, Chiara's tears were dropping on Anna's head, and for a moment, Chiara almost laughed when Anna looked up. Joseph helped Chiara get Anna to the couch, which was facing the coffin.

Visitors were lining up to view the coffin in a line that went out the door into the hallway and the viewing room across the hall. When Jack and Margo finally reached the coffin, Margo clutched Jack's arm, covered her mouth with her laced, perfumed, and initialed hankie, and began to cry almost hysterically. Jack tried to hide his shocked look and helped Margo kneel at the side of the coffin.

Jack whispered, "What is wrong with you?"

"What do you mean? I always liked your father. He seemed to be the only one nice to me."

Jack was surprised at the level of remorse Margo was showing and felt guilty for what he had done earlier by pulling her into the storeroom. He gently put his arm around her shoulder. "Come on. People are waiting."

Jack helped Margo up and walked her over to his mother. Margo hugged Anna, offering her condolences as everyone watched. Some quietly questioned if it was all an act. But if it was, it was a pretty convincing one. Jack guided Margo into a chair behind Anna. All of Anna's sons and daughters and their spouses had offered their condolences and were now sitting next to or behind her.

Joseph stood to the right of the coffin and greeted the guests as they approached. After seeing that Anna was being taken care of, Chiara joined Joseph. After a few minutes, Jack came over and pulled Chiara aside.

"Do you have any idea how many will come to Johnny's after the cemetery? Look at all these people already. This is the first day and they keep coming in."

"I don't know, seventy-five, a hundred? Why are you worried about that *now*?"

"Look at all these people. We have to pay for people even if they don't come," Jack replied.

"What does it matter? What did Momma tell you? We have the money. Maybe we can try to keep a count by asking people if they are coming to the cemetery. No, wait. Don't do that, it seems rude. We'll just have to see. I'll talk to one of the funeral directors to see how other families handle it. I don't remember what we did for Pietro. Oh yeah, it was at the house. Complete chaos. We'll never do that again."

Jack just nodded and went to sit with Margo. When Jack left, Joseph walked over to Chiara. "What was that about?" he asked.

"He wanted to know about the repass at Johnny's but we already took care of it so I just told him everything is ok."

Suddenly the sound of a woman screaming broke the low hum of people softly talking. Anna looked over toward the coffin, but couldn't see anything with all the people in line.

Chiara grabbed Joseph's arm. "My God! What the hell was that?"

"Wait here."

Joseph excused himself to get through the crowd. By this time the screaming had died down. After a few seconds, Joseph went back to Chiara who was by this time talking to some people that she didn't know, but tried not to let on that she didn't remember them. She excused herself and quietly asked Joseph what the screaming was all about.

"It was Mrs. Viola and a couple of other women that I don't know,"

Joseph said.

"My God. They must be her sisters and sisters-in-law. They've known Papa and Momma ever since they moved to Clifton. Papa helped one of their sons who was in big trouble."

Before Joseph could ask *what trouble,* Chiara spotted Anna's sisters, brother, and nieces from Buffalo who were heading toward them. Even though Joseph had met them years ago on their way home from their Niagara Falls honeymoon, he didn't remember all of their names. Seeing how crowded it was around Anna, they took any empty seats they could find.

Joseph looked around the room. Only about twenty minutes had passed and the room was already full. There were people in the hallway and people in the downstairs smoking lounge. A constant whiff of cigarette smoke came up the stairs and permeated the hall and viewing room. A man lit a cigar in the smoking lounge but to the delight of everyone in the room, the funeral director came into the lounge and asked the man to put the cigar out or smoke it outside. The man was insulted and began to leave. A small clapping of hands followed. The disgruntled man said he would finish his cigar outside and he wasn't coming back, or so he said because he knew his wife would kill him if he didn't return.

Joseph walked into the hallway to see how Dean was doing. Junior was sitting next to Dean and they were talking about school to keep Dean's mind occupied.

"Dad, I'm going to go downstairs to talk to Aunt Janine."

"Ok, pal."

Joseph waited for Dean to leave before he asked Junior how his son was doing.

"He's ok. I guess it's the first person he knows that died." Junior watched Dean look into the viewing room. "It won't be the last. He is very bright. How is he doing in school?"

Joseph gave a little sigh. "He is bright but he gets bored fast and easily distracted. If he likes the teacher he does well. If not, it's a struggle. I don't know if it was the best thing to send him to parochial school, but you know Chiara. She wanted him to have a Catholic education."

Junior nodded. He also thought that with Dean's personality, sending him to a Catholic school was a mistake. Dean needed more of what public schools could offer with remedial programs if he needed them because, like his mother, he is high-strung and finds it hard to be patient. With over fifty students in each of his classes, it is hard to get the proper attention from the teacher.

"How are the other boys doing?" Junior asked.

"They're doing ok. They're very different than Dean. Dean wants to know everything and do everything, and the other boys don't show much interest other than TV and playing outside. But they're young yet."

Junior knew what Joseph was talking about. Dean was totally different. In many ways, he was mature for his age, but in other ways, he was still a child. Perhaps because he had to relate to his younger brothers.

Joseph looked at Junior. "Dean is either going to be at the top of what he does or just a dreamer. Chiara has told him since he was little that he is going to college, so he must get good grades. I think he is more clever than book smart if you know what I mean."

"I like Dean. I'll try to give him a looking after. We both have a couple of things in common. He likes to build things, and he loves music. I wish my son had those interests," said Junior.

A couple of seconds went by. Joseph looked at the family and people he knew and commented to Junior. "I look around and, knowing these people before the old man died, it is going to be interesting to see how things go on from here. Someone's death either brings out the best or worst in people and families. Knowing this family over the years, I can tell you, that within this family, the old man's death will bring out the worst. But I'm hoping for the best. I can see the 'wagons already circling,' if you know what I mean."

"I've been around most of them, and I agree."

As the minutes went by, there was both intermittent crying and some muffled, nervous laughter. New visitors came up to the coffin and then paid their respects to Anna and the Buonoforte family members. Everything seemed to be settling down when a man and a woman, a teenage girl and a boy in a wheelchair came into the room. The room quieted down and attention was on the newcomers. Joseph went over to Chiara.

"Chiara," he whispered, "who are they?"

"That is Stanislau Zallenska, his wife Elisabeta, and their daughter Betty."

"Who is the guy in the wheelchair?"

"That's Gerald."

"And...?"

"It's a long story."

"It must be some story cause the room got quiet and everyone is staring and whispering."

"It is, and I'll tell you later..."

Donny walked over to Chiara.

"Hey. It's almost after 4:00. How are we going to get these people out of here?" Donny asked.

"Go tell the funeral director to make an announcement. I told Momma that we would go to Mario's to get something to eat before we come back here, so just the family, but tell the Buffalo cousins to come with us. Joseph, why don't you take Dean and get the boys and meet us at Mario's? I'll go with Momma. Donny, can we come with you?"

Donny put his arm around Chiara and kissed the side of her head. "Of course."

Chiara looked around the room. "Is Dean still sitting out in the hall?"

"Yeah. Janine and some others came back upstairs, and they are with him. I was watching to see if he was going to go in, but he hasn't moved."

Chiara looked and could see him sitting next to Janine. "I think he's scared. He's never seen anyone dead before. Let's get Momma up and maybe everyone will get the hint. She must have to go to the bathroom by now. Donny, go tell the funeral director to make an announcement."

Donny said he would and walked out of the room, but was stopped by a couple of people.

Chiara went to Anna. "Momma, let's go the bathroom, it's almost after 4:00."

Without waiting for her to agree, Chiara tried to help her mother stand. Giusepina, who was sitting next to Anna, helped get her up, and they walked toward the door but were stopped before they even went a few steps. One of the cousins, Josephine from Buffalo, came over to talk to Anna, but Chiara wanted to get out of the funeral home as soon as they could.

"I want to get my mother to the bathroom. We are going to Mario's restaurant when we leave here if you want to come with us," Chiara said.

"Let me tell Carol and Jean. My mother, Aunt Mary, and Uncle Tony are trying to get to your mother. I don't know if they want to go back to the house or what. We'll go to the restaurant. I am sure they want to eat."

"Ok. Tell Joseph and he'll give you directions. It's about five minutes from here."

Chiara walked her mother, together with Giusepina, by everyone, avoiding eye contact. She was relieved to see the funeral director walk past her to make the announcement.

Anna pulled Chiara close to her so she could whisper to her. "Don't leave me alone with my sister Sarah, you hear?"

"Momma. Still? You still can't hold a grudge. It's been years and..."

"Ascolti. Listen to me. Do what I tell you."

Chiara knew when to keep quiet. On their way to the bathroom, they could hear the funeral director make the announcement.

"Ladies and gentlemen, this concludes this afternoon's viewing. The Buonoforte family wishes to thank everyone for their attendance. The viewing will commence this evening at 7:00. In the meantime, you can join the family at Mario's restaurant at 710 Van Houten Avenue, about five to six minutes from here. Thank you."

Chiara looked at Giusepina and tried to talk in a whisper. "What! Who the hell told him to say that? Everyone is going to expect us to pay. Where the hell is Donny?"

Out of the corner of her eye, Chiara could see Jack practically sprinting over to them.

"Oh, no. Here he comes. Get Momma into the bathroom."

Giusepina walked Anna to the bathroom and passed Jack, who was almost nose-to-nose with Chiara.

"What the hell was that about?"

Chiara calmly shrugged. "I told Donny to tell the funeral director to announce that it was time to leave. I am sure Donny didn't tell him to invite everyone."

Jack looked over at Donny, and Chiara could anticipate what Jack would say to him. Chiara grabbed Jack's arm hard and moved close so she could whisper in his ear. "Don't you say a damn word to him. What the hell is the difference? These people came to see Papa. *Lascia sta,* leave it."

She pulled Jack's arm to emphasize she meant business, and he calmed down.

"Go get your wife, pick up your kids, and meet us at Mario's. And I'm not kidding, Jack, don't say a word or make a scene or you'll hear it from Momma."

"I don't know what the hell has gotten into her. Momma was never like that," Jack said.

"Well, you better get used to it. She's alone and probably scared. Well, look at Mrs. Stracci over there. Everyone thought she was this quiet little Italian lady who lived in her kitchen. After her husband died, she kicked her son out because he didn't want to work and she doesn't take crap from anyone. It's the Sicilian way. The husband is the head, and the wife is the neck until the husband dies and then the wife takes over."

Jack looked at old lady Stracci. "Who is that guy with her?"

Chiara glanced at the man and whispered, "Oh, that's her 'friend.'"

Jack smiled, shook his head, and walked away.

In the hallway, Joseph thanked Junior for taking Dean. Then Joseph bent over to Dean. "Dean, do you want me to come with you to see your grandfather?"

Dean hesitated a minute, looked toward the viewing room, saw all the people leave, and then the coffin.

A sudden reflection of red flashing lights coming from outside caught Joseph's attention, and he moved over to the window. It was snowing and there was major traffic because everyone was trying to leave the parking lot. Another police car arrived to direct the exiting cars in some kind of orderly fashion. Then Joseph looked over at Dean, who hadn't said a word, and just stood there looking at the coffin from the hallway. He walked over to Dean, touched him on his shoulder, and sat next to him.

"Hey, pal. I was the same way when my father died. It was even worse because it was in our house, in the living room. I was a few years older than you are, but I was still scared. Could you imagine going to bed with a dead person in the living room, even if it was my dad? It took me hours to fall asleep and when I woke up, I slipped quietly downstairs and my mother was sitting next to my father talking to him. I went back to my room and waited for my sister to get me up and come downstairs with me."

Dean looked at his father and gave a little smile. "I think I watch too many scary movies."

Joseph returned the smile. "Maybe you do. Come on. Let's go. We have to pick up your brothers. By the way, I'm proud of how you took charge and got here."

Dean looked at his father and grinned. Joseph gently hit him in the back of his head.

"Don't *you* be so proud of yourself. You're still in trouble."

Joseph kissed Dean on the top of his head. To Joseph's surprise, when they started to leave, Dean stopped without saying a word, walked into the viewing room, and kneeled beside the coffin. As Dean was kneeling, looking at his grandfather, he could visualize Enzo sitting at the edge of the kitchen chair at their house, twirling the top of his cane with his right hand. He could also see his grandfather taking out his false teeth and teasing him and then rubbing Dean's face on Enzo's whisker stubbles. For a few seconds, he was on the brink of tears but controlled himself. After a few moments, Dean came out of the room. Joseph had already put on his coat and helped Dean with his. They walked down the stairs to the parking lot without saying a word. Joseph thought to himself, *Just like his mother.*

Chapter 2
Mario's Restaurant, Clifton, New Jersey

The first afternoon viewing ended at 4:30, which was thirty minutes later than scheduled. Until the funeral director made the announcement inviting everyone to dinner at Mario's restaurant, it was just supposed to be the immediate Buonoforte family members. The original plan was to have people come back to the house *after* the evening viewing. Earlier in the day, people started dropping off pastries, cakes, pies, bread, and platters of cold-cuts and there would be plenty to eat. Because the afternoon wake ended so late, there wouldn't be enough time to go back to the house, eat, clean up, and return to the funeral home by 7:00. Now plans had changed and they would have to entertain before *and* after the evening viewing.

Mario's Restaurant was only five minutes from the funeral home and it would give the family plenty of time to have dinner before returning. It was not only for convenience, it was also a very familiar and warm place. The Buonofortes had been going to Mario's since they opened in 1945 when it was first, a bar, and then the owners started making pizza. It quickly became their favorite place, of course, aside from Maria and Antonino's restaurant. Sometimes the family would just want something different to eat and some place different to go.

Over the years Enzo had become friends with the owners, the Barliari family. Their thin dough pizza was their specialty; different from the traditional thick Sicilian pizza. Sometimes it created family arguments about which pizza was better. Just like there are similar arguments about whether to call tomato sauce *gravy or sauce* or whose mother makes the better meatballs. These conversations could be more cantankerous than talking about religion or politics. Every nationality has its own cuisine and dining traditions. For Italians, food is almost a religion, with the momma of the house being the high priestess of giving love through her cooking.

Cooking was not strictly left to the mother. Many of the husbands cooked. Rita's husband, Dante, who came from a restaurant family in Genoa, taught Rita how to cook. She, in turn, taught Chiara. Maria's husband cooked in the restaurant and at home, especially during the holidays, now that the restaurant was closed for the holidays, thanks to Enzo.

After Chiara, Donny, his wife, and Anna arrived at Mario's, everyone else started to come into the restaurant complaining about the weather. Jack walked over to Chiara, who was standing by the coat check with Giusepina. Chiara turned her back on him, anticipating what he was going to say. Instead, he asked about his mother.

"Where's Momma?"

"Rita took her to sit down in the dining room. We were just talking about how Momma is going to live in the house by herself. I don't know what we're going to do. I can't stay there every night. You know she is not going to want to sell the house. Maria and Antonino have room to take her, but there is no chance. You know Maria."

Jack wanted to keep the conversation going so he could suggest selling the house, but he could see Chiara was getting annoyed. Chiara made Jack a little nervous.

"You have a lot of room in your house, Jack. Why don't you give Momma your sons' room and make them bedrooms upstairs in the attic? You have the room, Jack. You want to talk to Margo about it, or should we have a family meeting?"

Now Jack wanted to end the conversation. He was annoyed that Chiara would even be suggesting that Anna would move in with him and his family.

"Forget it for now. Let's start ordering," Jack said.

Chiara snapped back, "Well, something has to be decided because I can't stay there every night. Who's gonna take care of *my* family?"

Now Jack *really* wanted to change the subject, so he said, "Why did the funeral director make that announcement? How are we paying for this? I'm going to talk to him. He should pay the bill. We didn't tell him to invite everyone."

Chiara shook her head. "For crying out loud, Jack, inviting everyone wasn't intentional. They're just having pizza and antipasto. It wasn't Donny's fault. It was just a misunderstanding. What does it matter now? Just go. And leave Donny alone. Don't worry about the damn money. If people give money as a gift, we'll use that. Don't give Donny any grief, do you hear?"

Jack liked to bully Donny because Donny was the baby of the family and got a lot of attention. Donny almost died when he was younger and there was much guilt because only Rita's husband, Dante, realized Donny wasn't sitting on the curb with a stomachache. It was appendicitis. Dante got him to the hospital, probably saving Donny's life. Jack was also resentful because Donny was a lot more affectionate and fun to be with and close to his parents and Chiara.

Jack asked Chiara again. "Whose is paying for it?"

"What are you worried about? Momma is paying for it." Then she lost her patience and pulled his arm to follow her. "C'mon. Talk to your mother and leave me out of this."

Jack pulled away, saying he was going to find Margo and their sons.

Maria walked over to where Chiara was standing. Before she could ask about Anna, Chiara told her where she was.

"Maria, Momma is in the dining room. I want to talk to Rita to see if she heard anything more from Don Carlo's daughter."

Maria left without a word, and then Donny came over.

"Donny, who told the funeral director to tell everyone to go to Mario's?" Chiara asked.

"I told you. I just said to him that we were coming here and then we were coming back at 7:00. I never told him to invite everybody. Are you kidding!"

"Well, if Jack asks you about it, you just tell him that and don't take any of his crap. I'm going to tell Momma I called Mario's to see how many people they can hold in their dining room. They said there would not be any problem with accommodating the expected number."

She left Donny and went to tell her mother.

"Ma, I called Mario's before we got here and told them what the story is and they said they would be able to accommodate us."

"Don't worry about anything. I will pay and I will take care of Jack," said Anna.

"Ok, Ma. Where is Rita? I have to talk to her."

Before Anna could answer, Jack came over to talk to Chiara and Anna. "Did you see all these people pulling into the parking lot? Who the hell told the funeral director to make that announcement?" Jack asked again.

Anna ignored Jack. She was in no mood to argue.

Chiara was losing her patience with Jack. "Ancora! Again! Jack, we just told him where we were going and he took it upon himself," Chiara said.

"Well then, he should pay."

"Jesus, Jack. Who cares at this point?! Momma is going to pay. Is that all you care about...or is it your wife?"

"Leave my wife out of it," Jack snarled.

"And what went on with you pulling her into the storage room?"

"Who told you that?"

"Everyone saw. You weren't very subtle about it."

"She was feeling faint, and I thought..."

"You are so full of shit! You think we're stupid? I really don't care. Just mind your business about the money. Go get your wife a drink."

Chiara walked away. Jack looked for a bartender, shrugged his shoulders, and looked for his wife and sons. After all the fuss, only about thirty people showed up. Dean and his brothers were occupied with everyone coming up to them, saying how big they got.

Except for the occasional yelling from Chiara for the boys to sit down, things were pretty quiet.

"Dean, don't tease your brothers. Grow up and act like an adult."

Some of the men were at the bar drinking and smoking. To save time and money, instead of having everyone order from a menu, antipasto, pizza, and mussels were ordered. Of course, a few people, like the relatives from Buffalo, wanted to order from the menu. Chiara said it was alright. What else could she do? Chiara was standing in the doorway of the dining room, hoping no one else was arriving. Joseph came over to stand next to her.

"Are you going to eat anything?" he asked.

"I can't eat. You eat and make sure the boys eat. Also, make sure my mother gets something."

Then they both saw Stanislau pushing the wheelchair, with his wife and daughter following. Joseph whispered in Chiara's ear. "Did you know they were coming?"

"I told them to come. He was close to my father when they lived up the street. They were close friends at one time."

"What is their story? You said that you would tell me."

"He had a butcher shop on Knapp Avenue and lived above it until he bought a house up from my parents close to Randolph Ave. When my father opened his store, Stanislau helped my father by giving him meat on credit. They had a good working relationship. My father introduced him to his wife."

"Yeah. But who is the guy in the wheelchair?"

"You see his daughter?"

Joseph nodded.

"Years ago, she had polio and..."

Suddenly there was yelling in the bar. Maria came over to Chiara and Joseph.

"You better come over to the bar. Donny is having an argument with your husband's brother Jamie, and I think they're going to get into a fight," Maria said.

Chiara looked at Joseph. "What the hell is wrong with your brother?"

"How do you know it's *my* brother?" Joseph snapped.

"You're kidding me right," Chiara said.

Joseph didn't say anything. Chiara remembered she saw Joseph's brother and his wife in the hallway of the funeral home when she heard Jamie's cackling laugh. She was annoyed at how loud he laughed and when she was about to tell Joseph to go talk to him, Jamie's wife Marlena gave him a hard nudge in his ribs and he stopped. Chiara figured that Joseph's mother, Caterina and Joseph's sister Loretta, and her husband would be coming in the evening.

Joseph has two older siblings. His older brother Jamie and sister Loretta. Jamie, being the oldest, would bully Joseph and Loretta would protect Joseph. They weren't originally from New Jersey, but from up-state Pennsylvania, near Erie. They also weren't Sicilian but Calabrese, which was an already established rivalry between the Buonofortes and the Fontes.

Joseph's mother, Caterina, was very different from Chiara's mother. They came from two different areas of Italy and social status. It was said that Caterina's family had roots going back generations to the Hapsburg's rule in Reggio di Calabria, with the family name being Amedeo. This might explain Caterina's aristocratic stature and behavior. In 1860, Giuseppe Garibaldi conquered the Kingdom of the Two Sicilies, which was a kingdom in Southern Italy from 1816 to 1860, and ended the rule of Francis II. Caterina's family eventually left Reggio di Calabria for fear of any type of persecution, having lost their homes and real estate holdings.

Caterina and her husband Francesco left Italy for America in 1907, leaving Caterina's five brothers and sisters behind. They planned to send for them when Caterina and Francesco were settled in Pennsylvania, where they had friends who left Reggio before them. But on the 28th of December, 1908, a heavy earthquake hit Reggio and shook violently for thirty-one seconds. An estimated 25,000 people perished in Reggio; 27% of its inhabitants. Although she desperately tried in vain to contact them, Caterina never heard from her sisters and brothers, who remained in Reggio. It was feared that they were killed in the earthquake.

Not much is known about Francesco Fonte's family, other than he was a talented landscape artist and grew prize-winning roses. It is said he and Caterina met when he was a gardener on one of her family's properties in Reggio. Francesco died when Joseph was only eighteen, leaving Caterina a widow with their three children.

Although it would appear the Fonte's were a close-knit family, like other families, the Fontes had unique personality traits and different ways of looking at relationships. There was also a dark side they all share; a bad temper.

Loretta's temper was not as fierce as her brothers. Unfortunately, she sometimes suffered from migraine headaches. Loretta was warm-hearted, and a devoted wife and mother. Like Chiara and Joseph, Loretta and her husband have three boys, and although around the same age, their personalities are very different. The same goes for the Fonte and Buonoforte family personalities.

Except for Chiara and Donny, the Buonoforte children are not as warm as Loretta and Joseph. Joseph and Loretta share the quality of unconditional love for their children and the importance of family. Jamie shared that quality as well, but was affected by his service in the Second World War when he suffered from battle fatigue, which affected his relationships with his wife and children.

Aside from a temper, another trait the Fontes shared is a keen sense of humor. Like Jamie, Loretta has a "cackle" kind of laugh. When Joseph laughed, he would throw his head back and his whole body would shake. Even though they shared a sense of humor, Jamie differed from his siblings. One minute, he could be cracking jokes and the next he might throw a chair across the room. He was an enigma to his family. An enigma that Chiara had no patience for. Jamie found out early in her relationship with Joseph that Chiara was a force to be reckoned with if there was an issue. After a time, they built a mutual respect for each other.

Often Chiara would comment to Joseph, "I don't know how his wife puts up with him. I could never be married to that man." Joseph just laughed because he could imagine his wife tearing into his brother.

Loretta was more the matriarch of the family than her mother, wanting to keep the family together. When dealing with Jamie, it was sometimes like walking on eggs. When any of the holidays came along, Loretta would want her brothers and their families at her house. Almost always

Jamie would come late or not at all because he'd fought with his wife. Loretta picked her battles and Jamie would be kept in line until the next incident.

Joseph, being the youngest, was sometimes bullied by Jamie. Things got even more difficult with Jamie when he came back after the war married to a German woman whose family took care of him during the war. There were whispers regarding why she married him; perhaps just to come to the States?

Joseph took a deep breath and walked over to the bar, where Donny and Jamie were arguing.

"What the hell is wrong with you guys?"

Donny turned to Joseph, whom he always got along with. "Your brother has to make a crack about Sicilians? Who the hell does he think he is?"

Joseph looked at Jamie and if looks could kill, Jamie would be on the floor waiting for the coroner.

"My wife is upset as it is and you two can't have a quiet drink together? Cut the shit," Joseph commanded.

Jamie walked away.

"Donny, what did he say?"

"Oh, he made some crack about how when at your father's repass everyone cooked and it was 'more homey' and the families in Erie have more class. Shit like that."

"Christ. Just stay away from him."

"Me stay away from *him*!? Tell him to stay away from ME! He doesn't know how close he got to me knocking his block off. Tell him to stay away from *me*."

Joseph just shook his head, knowing that Donny was right, but he still had his family loyalty. When he got back to Chiara, she asked what happened.

"Jamie being Jamie. I told your brother to stay away from him."

"What about your brother staying away from *my* brother?"

"Are we gonna argue over this? Finish telling me about the wheelchair guy."

"Forget it. I'm in no mood now. They're bringing more food in. Go check on the boys and tell 'the big one' to stop teasing his brothers and to grow up."

Chiara looked at Dean and realized he *was* growing up. She might need his help because she had an idea. She felt she may have no other choice with what could be a solution to what had now become a big problem, but she had to talk to Joseph and she didn't know how he would react.

Chiara watched as Joseph was handing out pizza to the boys. Things were tense. She was well aware of Joseph's temper and knew when to back off. She learned early in their marriage that she had to control the level of any argument and the silent treatment didn't work. One time, when they were having an argument, and she refused to discuss the issue, she locked herself in the bathroom. Frustrated because she wouldn't talk to him, Joseph kicked in the door. When people saw the door, they knew to think before saying anything too controversial to Joseph. One minute, Joseph would lose his temper and the next second he would be apologizing.

As bad as his temper could be, he would never raise a hand to her. He was deeply in love with Chiara, and she with him. Also, being a strong Sicilian woman, she would not put up with his temper and he learned to control it. It seemed the only times they had an argument was when it had to do with Chiara's family, but usually things resolved themselves—most of the times. Joseph had his family loyalty, but Chiara's family seemed beyond reproach.

Chiara walked over to Joseph and the boys, served them another piece of pizza, and sat down. "Hurry up and finish cause your father has to take you back home and we have to go back to the funeral home." Chiara looked over at Stanislau. "I have to go over there and say hello to them."

Joseph lightly held Chiara's arm so she couldn't get up. "First, tell me who that guy is in the wheelchair."

"Later. There isn't enough time."

"No, now," Joseph said.

"Ok. Not in front of the boys. Let's go to the bar. Besides, I could use a drink."

Joseph got her a seat at a booth in the bar and went to order the drinks. Drinking was rare for Chiara and Joseph, but they both enjoyed the occasional J&B scotch and water. Joseph ordered the drinks, brought them over to Chiara, and sat close to her to hear the story.

"Ok. Tell me about Stanislau."

They both took a sip of their drinks and Chiara began explaining what happened.

"Stanislau had a successful grocery business, but he became a big drinker after his daughter got polio. He was very distraught, started drinking, and would meet his Polish friends at Johnny's bar. After a while, his friends realized he had a problem. Well, their next-door neighbor Mrs. Mareska had a son Billy who wanted to study medicine to find a cure for polio because *his* sister died from it. His father had a heart attack and died, and then it was just Billy and his mother. We are so lucky they came up with the vaccine for the boys. It is a horrible disease. Anyway, Billy would come over and work on Stanislau's daughter's legs and try to exercise them so the muscles wouldn't die. It was very painful but it had to be done.

"Anyway, Stanislau's wife never told Stanislau that Billy was doing it because he didn't like Billy. They would have arguments when Stanislau would come home drunk and give Billy a hard time if he was around. As things got worse with Stanislau arguing with his wife, Billy would hear the yelling and come over and tell Stanislau to leave his wife alone or he would call the cops. One time, he did call the cops and Stanislau said he would get Billy for it one day.

"Well, one afternoon Stanislau wasn't home and Billy was exercising the daughter's legs. She would lay on her back in her bedroom and he would move her legs toward her chest and it would hurt. Stanislau's wife was hanging clothes in the yard and didn't see Stanislau come staggering in the front door cause he knew his wife was in the backyard and he didn't want her to see him drunk. Stanislau comes into the house and hears his daughter crying from the pain. He goes upstairs and only sees Billy's back.

Stanislau thinks Billy is trying to molest his daughter, and he tries to grab Billy. Stanislau is yelling and his wife comes in the house, runs up the stairs, and before the wife can explain…"

At that moment, Rita interrupts them.

"Chiara, Momma is asking for you. She wants to leave."

Chiara looked at her watch and saw it was getting late. If they didn't leave now people would arrive at the funeral home first and that wouldn't do.

"Alright. We have to go pay for the drinks," she said to Joseph.

"Wait. Finish telling me what happened."

Chiara saw their boys in the hall by the bar getting noisy and wanted to walk over and scold them. "Please, later. Take the boys home and I'll meet you back at the funeral home. My mother and I will go with Donny and his wife. I need to find Donny."

Joseph nodded, got the boys' coats, and helped zipper them up. "If you guys don't knock it off, I'm going to knock your heads together. Go say goodbye to your mother and grandmother and let's go."

Chiara saw Donny coming around the bar and called out to him. "Donny, Donny."

"Yeah, hold on."

Donny heard Marti Bonatti in the bar talking to the bartender and thought he should see what was going on. When Marti drank, he could get loud and obnoxious and this was not the time to make a scene. Donny walked back toward Chiara.

"Donny, listen. Joseph is taking the boys home. Can Momma and I come with you and your wife back to the funeral home?"

"Sure. Go find my wife. She's getting her coat. I have mine by the bar. I just heard Marti Bonatti over there and I want to talk to him. Here are the car keys. Do you mind just leaving now? I'll hitch a ride back with Marti and his wife."

"Ok, but don't take too long."

"Are you sure you're ok with driving in the snow?"

"Are you kidding!" Chiara laughed.

Chapter 3
Marti Bonatti's Story

For almost forty years, the Bonatti family lived a couple of houses down from Anna and Enzo. Although they were from Naples, which could sometimes be an issue with Sicilians, the families were very close. Marti's father worked for the sanitation department until he retired. His mother was a stay-at-home mom and a close friend of Anna Buonoforte. Marti married his high school sweetheart and was the star football quarterback for the Clifton Mustangs until he broke his ankle in four places. Instead of being bitter, he ended up as an assistant coach in his junior and senior years in high school. After he graduated, Marti started out as a policeman and eventually was promoted to police chief. Marti retired under suspicious circumstances.

When Marti saw Donny, he got off the bar stool, went over to him, and hugged him.

"Oh, Donny, buddy. I am so sorry for your loss. I loved your pop. He was a great guy. I was so upset when I heard. Heart attack, huh? When you gotta go, I guess that's the way to go. How about a drink?"

"A fast one if I can ride back with you."

"Sure. We have time. My wife said it's snowing hard, everyone has to clean off their car, they're all trying to get out of the parking lot, and it's a mess. We'll have a fast drink, for old times' sake. We should toast to your pop."

Donny knew it was hard to argue with Marti.

"Ok, Marti, just one, and a fast one, then I'll go back with you guys."

Donny walked over to the bar.

"Hey, Paulie, pour my *regular* and…Donny, what are you drinking these days? Um…Johnny Walker Black."

The bartender looked at Donny, who nodded, and then he poured two drinks.

Donny took the two glasses before Marti could grab them and handed one to Marti.

"Here's to your pop. A great guy."

They both took a sip and after a second, Donny almost spit it out.

"What the hell is this?"

Embarrassed, Marti switched the glasses. "It's ice tea. I stopped drinking a while ago."

Donny looked surprised. "Oh, oh, ok."

Marti was not going to give Donny any explanation; he just moved on. "Donny, your pop and mother are great people. We loved living down the block from you guys. After my father died, my mother didn't want to hear about moving. Finally, when she fell and broke her hip, we had no choice but to put her in the nursing home. That was the beginning of the end."

This sent a chill down Donny's spine. Before going to the wake, he was talking to his wife Dorothy about what was going to happen to his mother. With their five children, they had no room to take in Anna. Dorothy said she had a friend at the Paramus nursing home, but Donny wouldn't hear of it. He changed the subject.

"Marti, where's your wife?" Donny asked.

"She's here, probably blabbing with her friends. Remember her in high school? The most beautiful girl in the class. A real looker."

"I was a little young for high school then. After all the shit you put her through, you working late, worrying, and she still sticks with you."

Marti looked down. "Yeah, I know."

"And you got two great kids."

"Huh, great kids, sure. I break my ass and spend a fortune sending my son to college to become a lawyer, and what does he do now? He plays the fucking violin."

"What do you mean, just *plays* the violin? He's in the New York Philharmonic!"

"Eh, that's a bullshit job. What kind of job is that for a man? And those 'friends' of his...And my beautiful daughter; she marries this fucking bum. I told her not to marry him and what happens? He has a 'puttana' and leaves her with a two-year-old kid."

"I thought they got back together."

"Big deal. He's still a bum. But ya know...they *are* great kids and you're right; I am really proud of my son. We went to see him play. He had a solo, and he was great. The audience loved him. Ya know he calls us almost every day. Eh, what the fuck, it's his life anyway, and if he's happy...eh. Look at your pop. He comes here from the old country, works his ass off, has a bunch of kids, and then drops dead in the street."

Marti realized the harshness of what he said might have offended Donny.

"Shit, Donny, I'm sorry, man. But really? What the fuck is this life all about? Ya work hard and what happens? My old man dies, your old man dies, my mother dies, relatives die, friends die. I don't get it. What is the fucking point?!"

Donny looked down, shook his head, and changed the subject. "That was probably the last time I saw you and your family; at your mother's funeral. What was that, two years ago?"

"Two years and six months."

"Yeah. That's the last time I saw your brothers. What's going on with them?"

"Who the hell knows?"

"You guys don't talk?"

"Not anymore."

"What happened?"

"Eh. You know what happens with families when the parents die. I'm the oldest and shit happens. After my mother died and the inheritance was split up, they made up any excuse to just not be bothered anymore."

"Yeah, but you guys were close."

"Not really. There was always some bullshit. You know Vic is married to his wife's family. They kiss his ass and his wife has his balls in her purse so deep they're probably all shriveled up by now."

"Get the hell out of here!"

"I ain't kidding. They live with his in-laws in a two-family house and everything is about his in-laws. It all started when my father got sick and was dying when my mother and he were on vacation. Vic wasn't around because he was with his wife before they were even engaged or married. And as far as my mother, he didn't do shit for her. Everyone thinks his wife had something to do with it, but I also think he just doesn't give a shit. Oh, he made a fuss when he was with my mother, but it was all bullshit. His family would never spend a holiday with her. They would come either before or after the holiday. They have two kids that my mother hardly saw. Everything is his wife's family. Now that my mother is gone, he may have regrets, but it's too late. You have to kiss his wife's fat ass, otherwise, you're out. For years he didn't do shit for my mother and I figured, hey 'that's your thing.' I did what I did cause it's my mother and even though it would piss me off that my mother would never ask him to do anything cause he would disappoint her, I always figured it didn't matter. Also, I did what my father would expect me to do. Listen to this. When my mother was dying in the hospital, we were looking for a priest for last rites. The hospital finds a church that happens to be close to Vic and his wife. My bitch sister-in-law starts making friends with the priest, asking if he knew this one and that one, and my mother is *dying*! My cousins and I are looking at each other like, 'what the fuck!'"

"What about your other brother?"

"Oh, Joey. He helped out. He really got along with my mother and I thought we were close, but after a while, relationships just end even though ya want to have a relationship. When there's nothing in it for the other person, that's it, it's over. I was a dumb bastard thinking we were close, but I realized later that he didn't like me and wanted out. Then they make up shit so they don't look like assholes. What are you going to do? But even though my door is always open, they don't give a shit."

"That's weird cause I remember your parents were always great with you and your brothers."

"Don't matter. We're just different people. I'm not saying they're bad guys, they're just cold and resentful for whatever reason. The one thing I learned in life my friend is that some people, no matter how good you are to them, just don't like you. Call it jealousy, or whatever it is, they just don't and you have to move on and not give a fuck. Other siblings stick together but look what I got."

"We have the same thing with my brother Jack and his wife. Everything is her family. But there are times she is nicer than my brother but who knows if it's real. Now with my mother being alone who knows what is going to happen."

"Yeah, just wait for that. 'Buona fortuna!' Wait till things settle down. Then the real fun begins. Don't be surprised if they want your mother to sell the house and they stick her in a nursing home."

Marti could see that Donny felt uncomfortable and Donny quickly changed the subject.

"I did just see your brother Vic at the wake and he said hello."

"Yeah, I saw him when he was talking to your mother. He saw me and walked to the other side of the room. You probably didn't see his wife. It's all about her family."

Donny could hear someone walking near them with a clatter of high heels and he figured it was Marti's wife. Marti recognizing his wife's voice, stood up straight, fixed his jacket, and walked toward her with a *shit-eating grin.*

"There she is! My gorgeous wife. Isn't she gorgeous, Donny? I told you she is a looker. Didn't I say that, Donny?"

Donny turned to Marti's wife and kissed her on the cheek. "Hi Maggie, how are you?"

"I'm so sorry about your father, Donny. How is your mother holding up?" Maggie asked.

"Eh, she hides her emotions, but they have been together for over fifty years. It's gonna be tough."

"Yeah, they were devoted to each other like my parents."

She walked over to Marti and straightened out his jacket collar.

"Did you hear that, Marti? They were devoted to one another for all that time. Can you imagine that, Marti? For over fifty years."

Marti knew when his wife was being sarcastic and knew when to back off. He didn't deserve her and over the last couple of years he knew that if he didn't straighten out, he would lose the best thing that ever happened to him. Too many times his job came first, and then there was the drinking that went hand in hand with the job. Marti's wife took his arm and wanted to get moving. She took Marti's glass from his hand and tasted the ice tea.

"Good boy, Marti. Pay the man and let's go."

Marti looked at Donny and just shrugged his shoulders. Donny pulled out his wallet before Marti could.

"No Marti, I'll take care of this. Can I get a ride with you guys?" Donny asked again.

Marti's wife kissed Donny on the cheek. "Of course."

Marti put his arm around Donny as he was paying for the drinks. "Thank you, old buddy. Yeah, let's go."

Donny paid the bill and handed Marti over to his wife. "Here you go, Maggie. He's all yours. Let's get our coats. Come on Chief. So now you're retired, Marti. Why did you suddenly retire?"

Marti's wife spoke up before Marti could. "As far as him retiring, it was just time. Doc Conserva said if he didn't stop the drinking and with the stress from the job, he would either die from liver cirrhosis or have a heart attack, so he retired and I have him all day."

Marti laughed. "Yeah, lucky you!"

Donny got their coats and as they were putting them on, Maggie's friend came over and talked to her. Marti pulled Donny aside.

"You know about the drug bust that went bad and my best friend Benny was killed? We were warned by the drug gang they weren't going to tolerate any more busts. That's another reason I retired. I had enough."

"Yeah, Marti, what happened with that? How were you warned?"

"Some gang sent letters to the commissioner and me at the police station warning us to back off, otherwise there would be real trouble. We just thought they were bluffing. We never thought they would dare do anything so bold, but they did. By involving me in the investigation, we thought I was too high up in the chain of command to kill, but we never thought they would kill my former partner. When I heard about what happened, I was beyond livid. Everyone who knew me was well aware of my temper. I was warned multiple times by the commissioner that I better control my temper so I had no choice. I couldn't chance losing my pension or going to jail. What would that do to my wife and kids?"

"Do you know what really happened?" Donny asked.

"As much as I was allowed to know. Some facts, some rumors. I was retired when the investigations started to find out who killed Benny and then who killed the gang members. Things were intentionally quiet around the city. There were some suspicions there was a rat who was getting payoffs from the gang for information in city hall. It wasn't any cops. No way. It could only come out of the commissioner's office. False information was intentionally 'leaked.' Even though the people who were in the meetings were fully trusted, there were a couple who were under suspicion, so a trap was set up. You see, we had an informant on the streets who would give us information. We had to let a couple of deals go through so they would trust the informant. We knew we hit pay dirt when we gave out bogus information. This gave the gang a false sense of security and, through the informant, we knew the information made it to the street. We then narrowed down the rat."

They heard Marti's wife calling, so they walked over to her.

"Listen, guys. I heard they are trying to clear the parking lot, but a couple of cars are stuck. It's getting icy and they're throwing down salt. I'll stay in here. You and Donny let me know when we can leave. Donny, your mother, sister, and wife were able to leave and they know you're coming with me, so they will meet you at the funeral home."

"Thanks, Maggie," Donny said.

Marti and Donny went outside and continued to talk.

"Who was the rat?" Donny asked.

"I'll come to that. The informant found out that around Christmas the gang members were bringing in cases of liquor, folding tables, and chairs so the cops suspected the gang was planning a holiday party at an old, abandoned warehouse on the Passaic River on the Clifton, Passaic border. The problem was when? The cops knew the restaurants in town and figured maybe food for the party was going to be catered. Plainclothes cops would go to the delis and restaurants and ask questions from the help about business, and just by chance, one cop overheard that a big order was going to be delivered to the address of the old warehouse on Friday of that week. The dilemma was that they felt they wouldn't know who was going to be at the party and they didn't want to hurt any innocent bystanders. On the day of the party, four gang members were found shot by people arriving for the party and a couple of women were tied up and gagged in the lady's room. When people read in the papers or heard on the TV news what happened, details were scarce. The people 'in the know' felt certain it was some big cover-up. The newspapers didn't make much of the story and because it happened during the holidays, the story quickly died."

"So, then what really happened and who was the rat?" Donny asked again.

After Marti finished telling Donny what he knew, Marti went into Mario's to tell Maggie they could leave because the parking lot was clear but still icy.

Marti and Maggie walked out of Mario's. It was still snowing. Donny was behind Marti and his wife, and as he looked past Marti, he saw Marti's brother Vic at his car. Marti also saw Vic and hesitated for a moment.

"Listen, Maggie. Go with Donny. Here's the car keys. Go warm up the car. I have to talk to Vic for a second."

Maggie grabbed Marti's arm. "Marti, don't do anything stupid, please. Don't make a scene. We're going to a wake."

"Don't worry. I just want to say hello."

Donny heard the conversation and decided to hang back in case there was an argument or worse. "Hey Marti. Take it easy."

"No worries, bro, I just want to say hello to my little brother. Do me a favor. Help Maggie clean off the car and warm it up. I'll be right there."

Donny cleaned off Marti's car and came back to make sure there wasn't any kind of altercation between Marti and his brother. Vic was brushing the snow off his car and the brush got caught on the windshield wiper. He was having a hard time releasing the brush.

"Hey, little brother! Got a problem?" Marti asked.

Marti grabbed the brush, gave it a pull, and released it. When he gave the brush back to Vic, he saw Vic act surprised and nervous. Vic didn't know what to say. He rustled through his coat for his car keys.

"Marti, I have to get going. It's starting to snow harder."

"C'mon Vic. I haven't spoken to you in what...two years? Oh yeah. I had to work and couldn't go to your son's graduation party. Guess that really pissed off your wife, huh?"

Vic found the car keys, opened the car door, and stood behind it almost as a shield.

"What's your problem, Vic?" Marti asked.

"No problem."

"You're full of shit. If there's no problem, tell me why you didn't answer my calls. At least tell me to go fuck off. At least it would be more honest than your phony ignoring bullshit."

Vic wanted to get into the car but Marti blocked the door from fully opening.

"No, c'mon Vic. Just tell me to fuck myself. At least that would be honest and show you have some balls."

"Marti, I'm too old for this shit. I..."

"What the hell are you talking about? Who the hell do you think you are? You're too old for what? To talk? You're too old or you're too nervous cause you have nothing to say. C'mon, have the balls and the honesty to tell me to go to hell."

"Get out of my way, Marti."

"That's right. You haven't got the balls. They're in your wife's purse, so deep they're all shriveled up. Just grow another pair, Vic. C'mon, just tell me to fuck off so I can at least feel you're honest and..."

"Ok, ok...Just go Fuck off."

Hearing that, Marti clapped. "Bravo, little brother. Finally. Finally, some honesty and guts. Now what's your problem?" Marti could see Vic was nervous, and that was exactly how he wanted Vic to feel. "C'mon. This has to be more than not going to some party."

"Ok. Fine. You wanna know? You want some honesty? Ok. You know, Marti, you were always the golden child. You got whatever you wanted and did whatever you wanted to do."

"Now you bring that up? That is just bullshit."

"Yeah? You went to college. If you wanted to play the violin, you got a violin. If you wanted to play the piano, you got a piano."

"That's bullshit, Vic. You had the same opportunity to go to college. You went for what, one semester? It wasn't your thing. So what? Is that my fault? You had the same fucking opportunities I had. And you know why you didn't get a violin or whatever other fucking instrument? It's cause you have no fucking musical talent."

"I got no time for this shit."

"Here we go with you have 'no time for this,' but you have the time to make me look bad any time you have an opportunity, don't you? Whenever people say, hey how is your brother Marti? You don't think I know what you say? No matter what I helped you with or shared with you, you just don't like me. Just be fucking honest. You and Joey never liked me and it has nothing to do with me or what fucking instrument you didn't get. It's a bullshit excuse. After Dad died, I tried to help both of you with whatever you needed. When your place went on strike, who got you a job while you were outta work?"

That hit a nerve. Vic pushed open the car door, not caring if it hit Marti. Vic got into his car, but before he could shut the door, Marti held it open and faced Vic nose to nose.

"I don't give a shit if you hate my guts. I don't care if your wife hates my guts, or your kids hate my guts. By the way, I saw your daughter with your mother-in-law in the A&P a few weeks back. They hardly said hello. What the hell did you do, brainwash everybody? What the fuck did I do to them? You ruined everything for everybody. Shit. Why the fuck do I even bother? I hope you're happy."

Marti slammed the car door and started walking away, then stopped for a second. He could see people were watching them from their cars.

He turned, saw that Vic had gotten out of his car to clean the snow off his windshield again, and walked back.

"Just know this, Vic. All this bullshit has nothing to do with me. It's you and that other jackass brother, Joey. And it has nothing even to do with your wife. If you had the balls to stand up to her and if you had any problem with me, you could have come to me, but you never did. You didn't want to. Instead of having my back, you stabbed me in the back. Even so, my door is always open. That is what our parents would want, but you are so filled with resentment you, and that other phony jackass Joey, can't even be honest. I wanted two brothers and look what I got."

Donny called Marti to come to the car because they wanted to leave for the funeral home. Vic got into his car and watched Marti walk away. Vic looked at himself in the rearview mirror and slammed his hands on the steering wheel, cursing. He knew Marti was right about everything. He opened the car door and yelled after Marti.

"Marti, wait! Wait, a minute!"

Marti was going to ignore Vic but decided to stop and turn around. As he did, a car he didn't notice came toward him, and couldn't stop.

"What now, Vic? More bullshit?"

"MARTI! LOOK OUT!

A second later, a big black Cadillac slid into Marti and knocked him over, hitting his head hard on the ground. People saw what happened and started screaming. Donny ran over to help Marti. Vic was frozen in his tracks not knowing what to do. Maggie, seeing the commotion, walked over to Donny. She saw her husband on the ground and knelt next to him, trying to see if he was alright.

"MY GOD! MARTI, MARTI. SOMEBODY HELP! CALL AN AMBULANCE!"

A man ran over, said he was a doctor, and told his wife to call for an ambulance. "Please don't move him until an ambulance comes," the doctor said.

Donny took off his coat to cover Marti. Then Maggie saw Vic standing there. She wanted to kill him because she knew all the anguish he had caused her husband. And now this.

"IS THIS MORE OF YOUR DOING YOU BASTARD!"

She lunged at Vic, but a of couple people stopped her. Vic was dumbstruck and couldn't speak. Then she looked back at Marti and asked the doctor. "Oh God, please tell me he's Ok. Please, dear God."

Donny held Maggie as she was bending over Marti. Donny looked over at the car that hit Marti. It looked like it was backing up to get away. He got up and ran over.

"HEY! STOP!" Donny shouted.

The car stopped, and he opened the car door. "Where do you think you're going, lady? You hit that man!"

"It was an accident. I was just trying to get my car out of the way," said the driver.

"Lady, back up over there." He closed the door and directed her where to park. When she stopped, he opened the car door. "Put the car in park, give me the keys, and wait for the cops.

Donny could see there were other very well-dressed old people in the car. He closed the door. Both an ambulance and a police car pulled up. Donny signaled to the cop to come over. The cop came over with another younger cop.

"Sir, you saw what happened here?" asked the older cop.

"This old lady hit my friend and I think she was trying to get away," Donnie replied.

The older cop tapped on the car window and asked for the woman's license. She rolled down the window, got her license out of her purse, and handed it to him. The cop read it, then both cops walked back to the police car. Donny followed them.

"Sir. My name is Donny Buonoforte. I'm a witness. What's gonna happen?"

"Ok, sir. I'm Officer Mario Trieste. Go give your name and contact information to Officer O'Leary over there and if we need anything, we will call you."

"You're not going to arrest her?!"

"We're taking care of it, sir. Give your statement and contact information to Officer O'Leary and then go about your business or I'll arrest *you* for obstruction."

"She hit that guy!"

"I know, and you don't know who she is," said Officer Trieste.

"What does that matter?"

"It might matter."

"Do you know who she hit?"

"We'll find out."

"Well, *officer*...She hit former Police Chief Marti Bonatti!"

The startled cops looked at each other. "The Chief?" Officer Trieste asked.

"Yeah, the Chief."

Officer O'Leary shook his head.

"Shit. He helped me get on the force years ago. Shit. We have a problem. Read this." Officer Trieste handed the old lady's license to Officer O'Leary.

"Holy hell," said O'Leary.

Officer Trieste took the license back and shook his head. "Yeah...holy hell. Antoinette Genovesse. Sonny Genovesse's mother."

Donny knew the name but didn't give it much significance. "Who is Sonny Genovesse?"

Officer O'Leary looked at Donny with some surprise. "Don't you read the papers?"

Officer Trieste broke in. "Look, sir, we will call you if there is any need to talk to you. It's snowing harder. Please be on your way."

Donny ran to the ambulance as they were putting Marti inside and saw Maggie crying, trying to hold Marti's hand and being asked to move.

"Maggie, go with them. Call me at the funeral home and please let me know what is going on. I gave the police my number cause I saw what happened."

Maggie was crying so hard she couldn't respond and just nodded her head.

Donny hoped Maggie had left the car running so he could get back to the funeral home.

Chapter 4
Dean Has Doubts

As Joseph and the boys were finally able to leave the parking lot, they heard an ambulance getting closer but, they couldn't see anything and drove off. It was stone silent in the car. Joseph looked over at Dean, who was just staring out the window.

"Dean. You, ok?"

"Yeah. I was just thinking about...what's the whole point of everything?"

"What do you mean?"

Dean looked over at Joseph.

"Grandpa came here, worked, had kids and everything, and then he just dies. It doesn't make sense."

Joseph wasn't surprised at Dean's perceptive observation about something that has been baffling the brightest people for centuries. He wondered if he should give Dean the religious or the *real-life* explanation.

"Well, it is just what we do. What do the nuns at school teach you?"

"Yeah, they talk about heaven and hell, but everything still doesn't make sense. Why not just skip life and go to heaven instead of stopping off here?"

Joseph gave a little laugh, but he knew Dean wanted an honest answer. He was old enough to understand death and its consequences.

"You know my father died when I was a little older than you. I was eighteen. I was really mad because he was a good guy and you would have liked him. Like your grandpa, at first, it won't seem real. Then, after a while, you'll miss him. It never gets better. When my father died, I felt empty, like something was missing. It's like a piece of you is missing that no matter how you try, that piece will always be gone. It's like losing a leg or an arm. Yeah, you have another one, but nothing can make up for the lost arm or leg. I had your nanna and my brother and sister, but it didn't matter."

Dean was half listening, again looking out the side window at the snow, wondering when it would melt and looking forward to not having to go to school tomorrow.

"I guess so. But why go to school, why get a job or anything? I'm just going to die, anyway."

"We are all going to die, but life can be wonderful and it is what you make of it. We go around once, so why not make the best of it? Have goals. Establish good relationships. Get an education, get a good job, get married, and have kids. There is a lot to live for."

"I guess."

Joseph felt he really hadn't gotten through to Dean. Maybe he was too young and immature. Or maybe he was just smart beyond his years. Maybe he was beginning to understand life but didn't like what he was experiencing so far. Joseph realized Enzo's was the first of many deaths to come. Chiara, being the seventh child, had all her brothers, sisters, and their respective spouses older. Dean may witness all their deaths and the resulting loss. Joseph realized he must prepare Dean for the realistic facts of life, regardless of how dark. Then he thought about himself. Would he always be there for his boys? He discarded that thought and decided to just talk about the present. He continued his life discussion with Dean.

"What I believe is that living is like going to school. There are things we learn and take with us when we die. And then maybe we just keep coming back until we learn everything we need to learn. But we also should remember for this life we only go around once."

Dean turned and looked over at his father for a second, then back out the window. He remembered what happened the other day when they got the call his grandfather had died. Dean took the call and handed the phone to his father. He saw the expression on his father's face. Then he remembered when his mother came home and the bloody screams when his father told her. It was something he would never forget. He wondered how long that vision of his mother crying hysterically and his father helping her into the bedroom would haunt him. The muffled crying seemed to last forever.

Joseph looked over at Dean.

"Dean, what is it you want out of life?"

"Well, there are a lot of things I want to do. I know I want to travel. And I love music. I guess I will figure it out like everyone else. But I know one thing for sure, I'm gonna be a millionaire."

Joseph laughed but felt somewhat relieved that Dean had hopes and aspirations.

"See. You have goals. Now you need to have a plan to make it happen. Remember, you only go around once, so you must make the best of the time you have."

Joseph reached over and squeezed Dean's shoulder to show he supported him and was proud of him. From the back seat, one boy asked Joseph a question.

"Hey, Dad. What do you mean, 'we go around once?' Like a merry-go-round at Palisades Park?"

Joseph laughed. "No. Not like that. Don't worry. I'll explain it to you another time."

Chapter 5
The Johnsons

Joseph had just walked into the funeral home after dropping off his sons at home. He saw Donny run up the stairs, all out of breath. "Hey Donny, you better cut down on the smoking."

Donny ignored the comment

"You're not gonna believe what just happened."

"What?"

"As we were leaving Mario's, Marti Bonatti got hit by a car in the parking lot by some old lady."

"Geez."

"Marti hit his head, and I think he's in bad shape. His wife is going to call when she has more information. And guess who hit him?"

Before he could even guess, Donny blurted it out.

"Antoinette Genovesse. Ya know. Sonny Genovesse. The gangster. His mother."

"Yeah, I know who he is. My God. What's gonna happen?"

"I don't know. The cops were freaking out when they found out it was Sonny Genovesse's mother and then they freaked out even more when they found out it was Marti Bonatti, *The Chief,* who was hit. Before they realized who got hit, I think they were gonna call the old lady's son and hush it up. But it seems Marti got the younger cop into the force and, of course, Marti is a former cop...the former police chief."

At this point, Joseph really didn't care what happened.

"Where's my wife and your mother?"

"They are already inside. Now I'm freaking out cause I gave the cops my information," said Donny.

"You saw the whole thing?"

"Yeah, it happened so fast."

Again, Joseph didn't want to show his interest and changed the subject.

"I better see if my wife and mother-in-law are settled in."

As Joseph walked toward the viewing room, Howard Johnson, his wife, and two sons saw Donny and stopped to offer their condolences, then they approached Chiara and Joseph and did the same.

"Of course, you know my husband, Joseph," Chiara said.

Howard's wife Della shook Joseph's hand.

"Yes, Della, it's been a while," Joseph said.

"Oh, of course. We last saw each other during the summer at Nash Park with your children. I wish we were meeting again under better circumstances."

Chiara saw Anna was looking for her from the doorway. "Yes. Please excuse us. My mother wants to go inside and sit down."

"Of course," Howard replied.

As they walked toward Anna, Chiara and Joseph saw some people staring at the Johnsons and whispering.

Joseph leaned over and whispered to Chiara, "What the hell is wrong with these people? Didn't they ever see colored people before?"

"Shhh...The hell with them. The Johnsons are better people than half of the people in this room," Chiara said.

Joseph looked around and nodded.

"Well, things with colored people are going to change. You read about Martin Luther King in the Herald News and you asked me about him. The colored people, especially in the south, have been oppressed forever. Things are going to change and I think it's going to get messy. It's like a tinderbox waiting to explode with just a couple of incidents setting it off. I remember when Howard talked to your father about what was going on with the civil rights March in Albany. Howard is nervous things might happen around here."

Chiara was also nervous because she had read what was going on with civil unrest. She replied, "My father always said the colored people get treated like some of the Sicilian bosses used to treat their own people, but this is worse. Because of their skin color, they can't hide or run away. You know all those stories my father used to tell us about the good times he and Howard had when they worked in Little Italy? No one in this room would dare to say a bad word about the Johnsons. Even though my father is gone, I hope that won't change."

"I wouldn't think so. They are established in the neighborhood," Joseph said.

"Yeah. We'll see. By the way, did you get the boys in bed and did you warn Dean to behave and get to bed by 10:00?"

"I am not telling you anything until you tell me the rest of the damned Stanislau story!" Joseph replied.

Chiara tried not to laugh and went over to Anna. Instead of going over to the coffin, Anna had asked to sit down with Maria's help.

"I wanna sit here for a few minutes. Let Howard and his family sit with me.

"Sure, Momma. Are you ok?" Chiara asked.

Anna didn't answer and instead asked Maria to call Jack over to her. When he arrived, Anna said, "You bring Howard and his family over here and make sure they sit with me on the couch."

"Oh...Ok, Ma."

Jack approached the Johnsons, who had found seats at the back of the room, and he told them his mother wanted them to sit with her. They were surprised and got up and walked over to Anna. Rita and Giusepina had just gone over to sit next to Anna, but Anna told them she wanted the Johnsons to sit with her. Rita and Giusepina rose, greeted the Johnsons, and gave their seats next to Anna. The Johnsons tearfully offered Anna their condolences. Della sat beside Anna and held her hand. Everyone in the room knew exactly what that meant. Margo saw what was going on and enjoyed the sight. She got up and walked over to Chiara, who was standing at the front of the room with Joseph.

Margo whispered to them both, "Hmmm, Jack who dislikes colored people, Puerto Ricans, and queers escorted the Johnsons?"

Chiara whispered back to Margo, "It's my mother who told him to. Besides, it will make them feel more comfortable; it also sends a message."

"Clever woman. Brava, Momma!"

After Margo went back to her seat, Chiara went over to her mother to see if she needed anything. She saw Donny walk over to Joseph in the back of the room and wondered what they were up to.

Chapter 6
The Rat Revealed

Chiara joined Joseph and Donny. "I heard Marti was hit by a car. Is he alright?"

Before Joseph or Donny could answer, Rita came over to them.

"Chiara, Momma wants you. She wants to find out about the bill from Mario's."

Chiara hid her annoyance and went with Rita.

Chiara, what was that all about?" Rita asked.

"Marti was hit be a car in the parking lot of Mario's."

"My God. What happened?"

"I don't know all the details. That is what I was trying to find out."

Chiara and Rita went to Anna to discuss the bill from Mario's. Joseph and Donny walked out to the hallway for privacy since more people were arriving.

"So, what's the rest of the story Marti told you?" Joseph asked when they found a spot where they could be alone.

"For a couple of seconds, I thought Marti had been hit intentionally because of the story he told me. Then I saw who was driving the car, and I knew it couldn't be that."

"Donny, what story are you talking about?" asked Joseph.

"It's those rumors about the warehouse killings." Donny moved closer to Joseph so no one else could hear. "Marti's partner, Benny, was killed in an undercover drug bust that went wrong. Marti wasn't there because he was on the other end of town tracking the guys who were going to the drop-off point where Benny and the other guys were, in some low-rent apartment in Passaic."

"You're kidding?"

"I just told you. Marti told me as we were waiting to leave Mario's. I think most of it is true cause even though he was retired during the investigation, he had access to the info. They had even brought in the FBI because it was a drug case that had international connections or something. Anyway, the undercover plan was that Marti's group would call Benny at the drop-off point when the guys were on their way to make the drug sale. Except the phone is busy. Benny's dumb bastard partner is using the phone because he is panicking. He's on the phone to the station and it's taking too long waiting to talk to someone. Marti is trying to call Benny, and the bitch operator wouldn't cut in on the call to warn Benny and his partner that the drug dealers were on their way. They send an undercover car and now they scramble with what to do. No call is coming in and now Benny is trying to figure out what is going on and the other undercover guy is starting to really panic. Two guys arrive with the drugs and meanwhile, there are FBI officers on the roof with rifles. One of the neighbors, some old lady, heard a noise in the hall and cracked her door open. The drug guys were arguing about whether they should leave and they asked the old lady if she saw who went into the apartment. She said she didn't know, but she heard arguing in the room. The two drug guys try to listen at the door and then the phone rings to warn Benny and his partner. One guy wanted to leave cause he said he thought the men in the rooms might be cops cause they didn't have an accent, like the guys who made the deal. The other guy didn't want to leave cause he had the drugs, and he wanted the money. When the door opened, the drug guys figured it was a set-up and shot Benny and his partner and then they ran out of the building from the back door. The snipers were on the wrong side of the roof because they were waiting for the drug guys to come out the front. The two drug dealers were the ones from the same gang that Marti was going after. Marti felt guilty because Benny told Marti that morning that he wasn't cool with the drug sale and wasn't crazy about working with the other undercover agent. Marti told him not to worry cause the FBI was involved."

Joseph broke in. "So...what happened to the guys who shot Benny?"

"Wait. I'm coming to that. The FBI and the other investigators questioned the old woman in the next apartment, and she described the two guys she saw in the hallway. She said she would testify if she identified them from mug shots. A week later they go to talk to the woman again with mug shots and she was gone. She had moved out and nobody knew where she went."

"Then what happened?"

"There was this warehouse on the Passaic River where the gang got killed two weeks later, right before Christmas. There was going to be some kind of Christmas party."

"Marti told you all this?"

"Yeah. Unbelievable."

"How did Marti know all this?"

"Marti *said* he read the police report, and he talked to some of the investigators. You know they all stick together. They have to. There were four masked guys. Two of the masked guys took two women who were at the warehouse and locked them in the bathroom. They were screaming and cursing. They hit one of the women and knocked her out because she tried to attack them. The other woman got scared and just shut up. She hears everything that goes on and later tells the cops what happened. The four masked guys lined up the gang members on their knees, facing the back wall with their hands up. One of the poor bastards starts crying and the other three yell at him. It turns out it was this guy, Bats, his two brothers, and a cousin. The masked men tell Bats to get up and that he should have listened when they warned the gang to stay away from Clifton, or something like that. Two masked guys each hold a gun to Bat's head, hand him a loaded gun, and tell him to shoot the other three guys one by one. Said they'd let him go if he did. *Then*, the son-of-a bitch shoots them, one by one! The guys are screaming and begging Bats not to shoot them. They couldn't believe it! Bats shot his two brothers and the cousin! When it's all over, Bats asks if he can go. Bats is shitting bricks and he tries to talk his way out by ratting on the dead guys. 'Listen man. It was those other guys who shot Benny. I wasn't even there, man! Please, let me go!'

"They tell Bats to leave and as he is leaving, one of the masked guys shoots Bats in the ass. He's screaming in pain on the floor and another masked guy says, 'what kind of bastard would shoot his own people, you scumbag.' Bats is still on the floor when yet another masked guy says, 'should've stayed out of Jersey,' then he shoots him in each foot, then in his throat; waits a few seconds, and shoots him in the head. Just then, they hear a truck pull up and it's the caterer. They run out and tell the caterer that the party was canceled. And that's it. That's how it happened. At first, of course, everybody thinks it's Marti and some other cops, but they all were each other's alibi playing cards at Johnny's Bar, with Johnny as an additional witness."

Joseph gasps. "Holy shit!"

"Yeah, holy shit. And guess who the rat was? A secretary who worked in the commissioner's office. She was the only one in the police chief's and the commissioner's meetings who could have known what was going on. She was the only person who could be the rat. So, they sent out false information and then they also bugged her phone. She was somehow involved with one of Bat's gang members. After the killings, she disappeared. She just didn't show up to work and when the cops when to her house, she was gone with all her clothes.

Joseph asked again. "How did Marti know all this?

"Marti has connections. He has a friend in the FBI and they did a lot of the deep investigating. Nobody knows if it was a rival Philly gang or the cops. Many people think it was Marti and some other cops. Like I said, they all have alibis for each other. Who knows? Don't matter at this point. I guess justice was done at the end."

Joseph shook his head in disbelief.

Chapter 7
Stanislau and The Boy in the Wheelchair

Seeing her mother was taken care of, Chiara walked over to Joseph and Donny. They heard people whispering and turning around. When they looked at the door, they saw Stanislau coming in with his wife. Joseph pulled Chiara to the side and whispered to her, "Ok. Tell me the rest of the Stanislau story."

"Ok. Let's go sit on the side there."

They sit in the back corner of the viewing room, and Chiara continues the story.

"I told you that Billy was upstairs in the bedroom exercising the daughter's legs and Stanislau thinks Billy was molesting his daughter because all he could see was the back of Billy. His daughter is crying and Billy has her legs up. Stanislau screams in Polish. His wife hears him and runs upstairs. Stanislau grabs the boy, but his daughter is screaming to leave him alone. He takes Billy and throws him out the window."

"No goddamn way!" Joseph reacted so loudly that Chiara hit his shoulder and told him to be quiet.

"Ok, ok, go on."

"Then, like I said, just as his wife gets to the room, Stanislau throws Billy out the window. It's summer, so the window is wide open and he throws him right out. His daughter and his wife are screaming and crying, telling him that Billy is helping his daughter exercise her legs. Stanislau suddenly can make sense of the situation and runs to the window. He saw neighbors screaming, and a car stopped. The driver got out of the car and tried to help Billy, but Billy was unconscious. They call the ambulance and the cops arrive and the neighbors tell the cops what happened and they arrest Stanislau, as Stanislau is trying to wake up Billy. Billy's back was broken with the fall and..."

Just then, Rita comes over and tells Chiara that Anna wants her.

Before Chiara can answer, Joseph pulls Chiara's arm.

"Oh, no you don't...finish!"

"Ok. Tell Momma I will be right there."

"Well, to make a long story short, Stanislau goes to jail and Billy is now crippled, but here is where the story gets strange. Stanislau was let out of jail after two months because he made a deal with the judge. The deal was that Stanislau would take care of the boy and his mother for the rest of his life; Stanislau's life. That meant supporting him and physically taking care of him. What made the judge agree was that Billy's mother had cancer, and she really didn't have any relatives here. Billy would be alone, and there was no way he could travel to Poland.

"How could they believe Stanislau? What if he took off and went back to Poland or wherever?"

"That's a good question we all had. We found out that the business and house and all Stanislau's savings were put in the court's name as a trust or whatever, but they made sure his wife and daughter were taken care of. They also took his passport and his driver's license."

"Wow. How were they able to get the judge to even consider such a deal?"

Chiara laughed. "My father never forgets a kindness. He called Don Carlo to help. That is all we know."

"Was someone paid off or threatened?"

"Does it matter?"

"Guess not."

"So, Stanislau stopped drinking and dedicated his life not only to his family but to Billy. Billy's mother died about a year later. By this time, Stanislau loves the kid and does everything for the kid. Billy forgives and grows to love Stanislau. Stanislau sends him to Paterson State Teacher's

College because Billy wants to be a teacher. He takes the kid to and from college cause the judge gave Stanislau back his license just for that. The judge had a cop record the mileage every week for a while cause Stanislau could only drop off Billy with his wheelchair at the school and pick him up every day. What is even more ironic was that, though crippled, Billy feels what happened saved both their lives because he was getting into the wrong group of kids. At that point in his life, Billy had no father, and his mother was too ill to really discipline him. Another twist was that Stanislau reopens his business and works so hard he can afford to get Billy the best New York doctors and has a physical therapist come in every week to work with him. Believe it or not, Billy is beginning to walk, but he still needs a wheelchair."

"Unbelievable. It sounds like a phony Hollywood movie."

"Well, believe it cause it's true."

"What about the wife and daughter?"

"That's even a little stranger. The wife left Stanislau to stay with her sister and she was going to leave and go back to Poland with her daughter, but Stanislau and the judge convinced her to give Stanislau a probationary period. They were all living together and the daughter and Billy fall in love and they are getting married when she turns twenty-one in a couple of months."

"It is unbelievable. Is this really true?"

"We're all going to be invited to the wedding. Go ask my sister Rita. She is good friends with Stanislau's wife, Stasia."

"No, I believe you, it's just that..."

"I will introduce you. Oh, another thing is that Stanislau is very smart. He got his high school diploma and is very interested in taking night classes at Paterson State in business management. Eventually, he wants him and Billy to expand the business if Billy doesn't want to be a teacher."

"Is this all true?" Joseph asked again.

"No. I really have the time to make it all up. Let's go. My mother is waiting for me."

Chapter 8
What Happened to Don Carlo?

Conte's Funeral Home parking lot was filling up fast and cars were lining up the street. The snow was letting up and people who worked during the day were coming for the evening viewing. Anna wanted Chiara and Rita to help get her to the coffin. Chiara was thinking to herself why Anna didn't ask Maria to help her. She was sitting right behind her. Suddenly, when people saw Anna, there was silence. When Anna got to the coffin, it was a repeat of the afternoon's viewing. Anna was screaming in Italian, but this time Chiara and Rita held onto her so she couldn't grab Enzo. They all understood why she was grabbing him. Enzo wasn't sick and because he died so suddenly, he looked like he was just sleeping.

For a moment Chiara remembered when her brother Pietro was in the coffin. Enzo tried to pull Pietro out of the coffin and was screaming. It was utter turmoil. Other people screamed, and Jack and the two funeral directors had to pull Enzo from Pietro. From that point, Jack or Francesco had to watch him.

As Anna was screaming, one woman standing next to Maria asked what Anna was saying. Maria was trying to hold back tears but answered her. "My mother is yelling at my father, saying that he wasn't supposed to die. She wanted to die first. They should have died together. Things like that."

Chiara and Rita got Anna to sit finally and things calmed down. Then Jack came over to Chiara. Chiara looked at Jack and pulled him aside.

"Jack, if you ask me one more goddamn time about how much the bill was at Mario's, I'm going to crack you one."

"No. I have to tell Johnny's about how many people will be there after the funeral."

"Jack, how the hell should I know? Look around. This is just tonight. Say a hundred, a hundred fifty. What the hell do I know?"

At that moment, Rita ran over to Chiara and before Rita could say anything, Chiara saw what Rita was coming over to tell her. Chiara stood silent and some people in the room whispered. Joseph walked over to Chiara and they both looked at each other. Even Jack was surprised. Rita said nothing and went to greet the group who had just walked in. Chiara walked over to Rita, shaking her head. Rita knew she wouldn't hear the end of it. Don Carlo was being wheeled into the room by his daughter with her husband next to her and on the other side of the wheelchair was Bruno Sessino.

Chiara greeted Don Carlo and kissed him on both cheeks. "Don Carlo. What happened?"

Before he could answer, Lucia explained. "I am so sorry I didn't call you back and explain what happened. There was so much confusion. My father insisted that he not go to the hospital. I was so upset because I thought we had lost him. He sometimes doesn't pay attention to his diabetes the way he should, and he goes into a diabetic stupor. But he is alright and insisted that he come here tonight and when my father insists on something, there is no changing his mind."

Chiara was holding Don Carlo's hand the whole time his daughter was explaining what happened. "Well, thank God everything is ok. We were afraid the worst had happened because the message wasn't clear. You should still see the doctor."

"Eh. Doctors. What do they know? My neighbor's a doctor, the president of NYU Medical or something. He said I was alright," Don Carlo replied.

As Chiara was explaining to Don Carlo's daughter about the miscommunication, she looked right at Rita for a couple of seconds. Then she kissed Don Carlo's son-in-law and Bruno Sessino. She whispered in

Bruno's ear that she wanted to talk to him when everything calmed down and everyone was settled.

Chiara led the small group to her mother. When Anna saw Don Carlo being wheeled up, she cried out and Chiara had to calm her. Don Carlo saw Anna and then Enzo in the coffin. He took a hankie from inside his jacket and cried as Anna hugged him. When Don Carlo saw the Johnsons, there was another explosion of tears from Howard and Don Carlo. The Johnsons moved off the couch so that Don Carlo could be helped out of the wheelchair and sit next to Anna. The Bunoforte children came over to pay their respects to Don Carlo and introduce their respective husbands and wives. It seemed to overwhelm him.

Chiara took Bruno Sessino, who looked surprised, to the side.

"Chiara, I've never seen Don Carlo cry. Even when he found out his wife died on the Andrea Doria. He kinda shut down for a while. The only one who could get through to him was his daughter. I never saw a man so dedicated and in love with their daughter like Don Carlo."

Chiara wasn't interested in how much Don Carlo loved his daughter or the last time he cried. She wanted some information. Information she had waited all her life to ask, but she would never ask questions while her father was alive. Enzo made it clear that the "past was the past."

"Bruno, we have a lot of questions about things that happened that we never understood, like why my mother had to come ahead of my father to America and a bunch of other things. My father was very close-mouthed but we feel we want to know. It's part of my mother's and father's history. It's part of their kids' history, right or wrong, good or bad. We finally want to know. I know my mother knows, but she told us to ask *you*. I hope it was nothing bad."

"Why do you have to know these things *now*? It's not that big a deal anymore. The past is the past," said Bruno.

"Because we also have some documents that need an explanation and something that we think may be dangerous to hold on to."

Bruno looked at Chiara. "You mean the Crucifix?"

"How did you know?" Chiara asked.

"Your father wanted you to know about the history of the Crucifix in case he died." Chiara looked toward the front of the room to the right of the coffin and Bruno whispered to her. "Chiara, in case I died first there are papers that will explain that would have been forwarded to you. He never wanted the church to get their hands on the papers. The Crucifix came into Enzo's father's possession under some mysterious circumstances, which we may never know about unless Don Carlo knows, cause I don't know. Maybe you should ask him about it. I will give you the papers after the funeral. It surprises me to see the Crucifix on a table next to the coffin. I don't think that was wise."

Chiara was stunned that Bruno told her it wasn't a good idea to bring the Crucifix to the funeral home. "My mother wanted it next to the coffin. She has no idea about the papers or anything."

Bruno ignored Chiara's comment. "Please remove it tonight and do not bring it back. Hide it in your home. If anyone asks why it isn't back, say you gave it to the church for safekeeping."

Chiara looked concerned and Bruno tried to ease her concerns and took Chiara's hand. "Don't worry. Along with your father's death, perhaps everyone who was connected with the Crucifix is gone. But don't give it to the church. Don't trust anyone with it. When you understand where it came from, you may decide to return it anonymously. I don't know if that is something your father would want, but you have to decide. I also know he only wanted *you* to have possession of it. You must decide. Talk to your husband. It affects you all."

Chiara didn't ask questions. She didn't want to know any more information, as she was already overwhelmed. She also thought it was weird that Bruno said "don't worry about it" but also said, "don't trust anyone." Was the conflicting information the rambling of an old man? Though she repeated in her head what Bruno told her; *don't trust anyone. Could she trust him or even Don Carlo?* For now, Chiara would go along with what he told her.

"Ok. I will take it and hide it and talk to my husband about it." She saw a man with a heavy wool coat who looked familiar and asked Bruno about him. "Who is that man? I saw him come to my parent's house a few times. He looks like the man who hid a car in our garage. I recognize that big scar on his face. My brother Pietro thought there was a dead body in the trunk. Who was my father hiding the car for?"

Bruno tried to hide his surprise that Chiara was asking about a *body in the car trunk.* He laughed, to the surprise of Chiara.

"Where did you get that from? There was never a dead body in a trunk in your father's garage. What was in the trunk in your father's garage was a crate one of his friends wanted him to hide because he took a case of baccala, you know, dried codfish. He didn't come back for a couple days and your brother Pietro goes into the garage and smells the fish and thinks it's a dead body. He just let his imagination run wild. We had a good laugh about it."

Chiara didn't know if she could believe him because the two people who could confirm the story were gone. Why would someone hide a car that had fish in the trunk? Did he steal the fish? Also, it wasn't the first time a car was hidden in the garage or that someone was hidden in the house in a secret attic room. She told Bruno she wanted to attend to her mother. She thanked him and kissed him on each cheek. *At this point, did it even matter?* she asked herself. Even though she knew her father wouldn't be involved in anything like hiding a dead body, it still bothered her.

There was nothing Bruno, or anyone else, could tell Chiara that would make her ashamed of her father or love him less. She knew what it was like surviving in Sicily or what had to be done to survive living in a new country where you don't really know anyone or if you could trust the Irish cops. Foreigners weren't wanted by the generation before them when *they* were the foreigners. Enzo was harassed and had to outsmart and protect himself and his family. Even though things changed after the war, some of the old prejudices and distrust lingered.

Instead of attending to her mother, Chiara looked over at Joseph, who was talking to a few people at the side of the room. That moment reminded her of how handsome he was. His dark blue eyes with his jet-black hair and that easy smile had melted Chiara's heart when she first laid eyes on him at her sister Giusepina's house. It was a blind date that both Chiara and Joseph kept wanting to cancel. She thanked God she hadn't. As handsome as he was, he was also warm and affectionate.

She took her eyes off Joseph and looked around the room. She knew she didn't remember everyone there, especially the old-timers. She knew most of the secrets of the old-timers she recognized. She knew who was cheating on whom, who were the bootleggers in the old days, and where the "so-called bodies" were buried. She knew because Enzo confided in her, and only her. He even confided how he felt about her brothers and sisters. Of all his children, Chiara was most like him. As he was passionate, she was passionate, as he was loving and self-sacrificing, she was loving and self-sacrificing. But it wasn't the same for Enzo's and Anna's other children.

Maria, the oldest, was mostly selfish and a bragger. Enzo said many times that if he didn't know his wife was faithful, he would think Maria was someone else's daughter. Giusepina was good and kind, but he felt closer to Chiara. His son Francesco was like his mother, aloof and hid his emotions, but then again, kind and loving. Both Enzo and Anna loved Pietro and trusted him, but when he died, Enzo had no one but Chiara. Rita could be loving, but also selfish and moody. Jack was the most handsome and charming of the boys, aside from Donny, but Jack was weak. Although some would say his wife was the problem, it was mostly Jack. Donny, the youngest, was much like Chiara, but he had a young family and Enzo never wanted to burden him.

Although it was never said, Enzo knew that if he died before Anna, Chiara would take care of her. And now the time had come. Once again, Chiara felt another family loss, like the loss of Pietro. Another piece of emptiness that would never be filled. Although giving the appearance of being strong, she was still vulnerable and fearful, especially when it came to her children. When Dean was about two-years-old he was grocery shopping with Chiara; seated in the shopping cart. He almost choked to death on the carrot she had given him. He got to where he was turning blue, but fortunately, he coughed it up. Yet, she never forgot it and it still haunts her.

Chiara pulled herself from her memories, found Joseph, and said, "Joseph, go to the funeral director's office and get the box the Crucifix came in and pack it up. We need to take it home."

"Now?"

"Yeah, I am just very nervous about what Bruno Sessino told me about it. He said he had some papers that would explain everything to give to me."

" *We* have the papers about it."

"Well, I guess there are more. He wants us to hide it in the house and if anybody asks, say we gave it to the church to hold so it doesn't get damaged.

"Oh Jesus, look who just came in."

Chapter 9
Marilyn Margenti

Chiara and Joseph looked at the entrance of the room. A woman with a full black mink coat, matching hat, and sunglasses was nervously looking around to see if she knew anyone.

"Who is that?" Joseph asked.

"Have you ever heard of Marilyn Margenti?" replied Chiara.

"You mean the *old* opera singer?"

"Yes."

"How does she know your family?"

"You know my father loved opera. You heard the stories a thousand times about how my father and Bruno Sessino used to either sneak in or he knew someone who worked at the old Metropolitan Opera House in New York. They used to sit in the mezzanine, bring wine and a sandwich in a paper bag, and watch the opera. My mother never wanted to go and besides, who would watch the kids? This was years ago."

"How did he know her?"

"He knew her before she was a star. She used to sing at the Mussomeli Feast in Passaic when she was young. Then she went to study in New York. When the star didn't show up to play Violetta in La Traviata, she went on as the understudy. My father and Bruno thought she was the best mezzo-soprano they had ever heard, and they heard a lot. Don Carlo's girlfriend, Angelina, was an opera singer and Don Carlo had connections. Bruno and my father thought Don Carlo could help her because she probably would never get a chance. Understudies rarely perform again, especially if they're good.

"How did your father get to know her?"

"At the time, my father was one of the organizers of the Mussomeli Feast, and he was the one who hired her. Then later, even though she was famous, she would perform at the feast for free for one night and afterward, he would bring her over to our house. We haven't seen her in a while because she left here to perform on tour for years in Europe. Also, her mother was a Sicilian and my mother cooked and reminded her of her mother, who was still living in Sicily. Come with me."

Chiara went over with Joseph to greet Marilyn. "Hi, Marilyn. I don't know if you remember me, but I am Chiara, Enzo's daughter."

"Oh dear, yes! I remember you. Che bella! You sat on the stage when I sang at the feast...the Mussomeli Feast. I used to come to your house."

"This is my husband, Joseph."

"Oh, how handsome!"

Joseph put out his hand to shake hers, but instead, she kissed him on both cheeks. Then she changed her tone in keeping with the situation.

"The years have gone by so fast. I am so sorry about your father. I want to see your mother. How is she doing?"

"As best as she can. There are a lot of people around her."

Chiara was looking for a way to get through the crowd, but she would have to wait and talk to Marilyn. "How have you been?"

"Well, I am sure you heard about my divorce. It was in all the papers. Thank God for Maria, who took me in. I had to escape to Greece and Maria and Aristotle let me stay with them. Then Maria arranged some performances for me in Italy, Greece, and London when Maria and Aristotle went on vacation. I helped her out performing at the La Scala in Milan and Covent Garden in London."

"How did you hear about my father?"

"Father Ludovico. I am going to perform at Catholic Charities for a fundraiser. He knows how close your father, Bruno Sessino, and Don Carlo were. I see that Don Carlo is sitting next to your mother."

"Father Ludovico will be here later to say prayers. How do you know

Father Ludovico?" Chiara asked.

"I met him years ago in Milan before the war when I was at La Scala. I was performing in *La Boheme* and sitting in the first row I saw this beautiful man. He almost distracted me as I first came on stage. Then he came a few nights later, and I wanted to meet him. My maid went to find him for me when the opera ended, but he had gone. I never saw him again until I went to mass at the Duomo. The priest saying mass looked familiar, and I thought, could it be him? To get a better look, I moved to the front row and there he was with another priest saying mass. I was gutted. After mass, I waited for everyone to leave and then I walked toward the altar. He came out of the Sacristy. I introduced myself, but of course, he knew who I was and was quite surprised. I asked him if he would like to have lunch with me and he reluctantly agreed. He knew what I wanted, really, but his being a priest put me off that idea. Anyway, we had lunch and then dinner a few times, and then my tour ended.

"We kept in touch as well as we could. He would always give me a forwarding address and I would tell him where I was performing. Then the war came and, of course, it was impossible to contact anyone. After the war, there was a fundraising benefit to repair La Scala because it had been bombed in the war. I was in Paris performing and I got a telegram from Father Ludovico asking me to come to perform at the La Scala fundraiser. Luckily, my contract at the Paris Opera House had finished, and I rushed down to Milan. A huge stage was set right in the piazza in front of the Duomo and an orchestra made up of anyone who was around or alive who had played at La Scala. It was a wonderful evening, and we raised enough money to repair the opera house. Then we could keep in touch. He knew of my relationship with your father, Don Carlo, and Bruno Sessino. Is Bruno here?"

"Yeah..."

Chiara looked around to find him. "He may be down in the smoking lounge. Let me take you to my mother and Don Carlo. There is finally some room. I will see where Bruno is."

Chiara led Marilyn to her mother and Don Carlo. Some people recognizing Marilyn began to whisper. Both Anna and Don Carlo were surprised and happy to see Marilyn. Chiara went toward the smoking lounge and saw Bruno coming up the stairs. As he came toward her, she pulled him to the side.

"Guess who is here? Marilyn."

"Marilyn who?" Bruno asked.

"You know, Marilyn. Marilyn Margenti!"

"Marilyn. How did she find out? I haven't seen her in years. The last time I knew anything about her, she was in Greece and there was a big scandal."

"Father Ludovico told her...and what do you mean scandal?"

"Her and Onassis. They were thought to be having an affair."

"Were they?"

"What I know is that some reporter made it up because when the affair was supposed to have taken place, Callas was with Onassis on his yacht in Monte Carlo and Marilyn was performing Carmen in Covent Garden, but it didn't matter. Marilyn said she wouldn't return to Greece because she would never do anything to hurt Maria. Onassis was so angry there was a rumor he wanted to get the Mafia to kill the reporter and the editor of the paper. The newspaper retracted the story and fired the reporter, but it didn't matter. The damage was done and the other reporters kept hounding both Ari and Maria. I think in some way it affected their relationship. Poor Marilyn did the right thing, but I don't think she was ever able to be with them in public. Don't ask her about it. In fact, I hope there are no reporters around. She took a risk coming here."

"Can you take care of her?"

"Yeah."

"Are you coming back to the house later?"

"Yes, I'll stop over."

Chiara and Bruno walked over to Anna, and Marilyn was happy to see Bruno. It was bittersweet because Bruno was in love with her, but she had run off with a tenor who didn't amount to anything and lived off of Marilyn until he died of alcoholism after she divorced him.

"Oh, Bruno! It's so good to see you. It is just under these sad circumstances," said Marilyn.

Bruno hugged Marilyn and whispered in her ear. "Marilyn, let me get you out of here before anyone calls a reporter."

"I don't care anymore. Time has gone by and I would again tell the truth. I am not afraid. Besides, Ari and Maria are being asked other questions. I'm old news."

"What do you mean?"

"Well, eventually it will be common knowledge that Maria is having trouble with her voice. I stood in for her a few times. Although she was grateful, I could sense the resentment. Their troubles have gotten worse, so of course I stay away. Even if a reporter would ask, I haven't been to Greece in years. There is also the visiting of the Kennedys if you know what I mean; Jackie and her sister."

Chapter 10
The Crucifix is Missing

People began to line up to pay their respects at the coffin, then to Anna and her family, and then leave.

Rita walked over to Chiara.

"Don't think I forgot about the message that Don Carlo died," Chiara said.

"Oh Jesus, forget about it already. Do you know how many people are coming back to the house?" Rita countered.

"I don't know."

"You didn't say anything to anyone, did you?"

"No."

Chiara looked at the number of people lined up and when some of them moved aside, she saw the Crucifix was gone. She didn't mention it to Rita, saying instead, "Stay here. I need to find my husband."

Chiara saw Joseph holding a box. She walked over to him as he was talking to a person who had just arrived. She took the box, which was empty, and pulled Joseph aside.

"What happened? Where is the Crucifix?"

"I was about to pack it up," replied Joseph.

"Where the hell is it? Who took it!"

Joseph looked at the empty table and his heart sank; he should have gotten to the Crucifix sooner. They walked to the funeral director's office and saw him going through some papers.

"Excuse me, did you take the Crucifix?" asked Chiara.

"No. My God. Didn't you take it?"

Joseph was losing his temper. "Why would we ask you if we had it?"

"I don't have it," said the funeral director.

"Shit! Who would have taken it? I have to get Bruno," Chiara said. Chiara tried to control how fast she was walking, not wanting to create suspicion that something was wrong.

"Excuse me. Bruno, can I see you for a minute?" Chiara led Bruno out into the hall. "The Crucifix is missing! Did you take it?"

"No. Why would I take it? I was the one who told you to hide it."

"Oh, my God. Someone took it. It's gone."

"You asked the funeral director?"

"Of course. He has no idea. What do we do, call the police?"

"That is the last thing we do. I don't know what else to do," Bruno said.

"Oh, Jesus."

"Yeah, Chiara. You can say that again!"

"Chiara, strangely, whoever took it may have done you a favor. Wait until you read the papers I have to give you."

"You know, we found papers too that my father hid away with his will and other papers."

"I guarantee. They're not like these, just because of where they came from."

"What do you mean?"

Bruno looked around to see if anyone was listening. "These papers are from the Vatican Archives in Rome."

"Come on Bruno. Are you kidding? What is this, the 'Maltese Falcon?'"

"I am telling you. Someone who had these papers died, and I got a hold of them."

"Who died? The Pope?"

"This isn't a laughing matter, Chiara."

"You mean all this time it was out in the open in my parent's bedroom and now suddenly it is valuable and dangerous?"

"That's right. Think about how your father got it. His stepsister brought it out of Sicily, right? I understand Enzo's stepmother had a fond affection for it and then it was taken. What I can tell you is that it was not given to your father by his father. It was stolen and ended up in your stepmother's hands. And where it was stolen from and when it was stolen has never been forgotten, and that is just the beginning. More than one person wants it back. Supposedly, it has a name. La Crusifix da Giello di Caprese."

Chiara was physically upset with the news and didn't care about the name. "That means whoever doesn't have it is going to try to find out where it is?"

"I am afraid so."

"Bruno, you have nothing to be afraid of, we do. Let's get back to my mother."

"Really? Really? Think again!"

As they were walking it suddenly hit Chiara, could Bruno be one of the people who wanted it? How does he know so much and how did he get the information? She never got an answer. *My God.* Suddenly her blood ran cold. As she approached her mother, Don Carlo got back into his wheelchair.

"Chiara. Come to the hallway," Don Carlo said.

When Chiara got to the back of the funeral home with Don Carlo, he looked straight at her. "I have the Crucifix. My chauffeur has it in the trunk of the limousine. He is sitting in the car with a 38 pistol under his coat. Don't worry."

"Don't worry?! It's being guarded by a guy who probably isn't really a chauffeur and has a gun?!"

"I said don't worry and aside from me and Bruno don't tell anybody about where the Crucifix is. Tell them you gave it to the church, don't answer any questions, and don't trust anyone."

"Now what?" Chiara asked.

"Well, we have to determine if the Crucifix is the one that was made for Pope Julius II by Michelangelo."

"What?!"

"Shhhh...you heard me. There were a couple of rumors. One is that it was stolen from the Vatican Museum by a disgruntled cardinal who was passed over a couple of times to be elected Pope. Another rumor is that it was stolen by one of Napoleon's men and given to Napoleon as a gift when he was in exile on the island of St. Helena in 1821. The other part of the rumor is that someone on the island poisoned Napoleon by giving him medicine that was really poisoned and stole the Crucifix during all the confusion, which is interesting because the cause of death has been one of France's greatest mysteries. Where it went from there, who knows? We only know it ended up with your father's stepmother."

"Jesus."

"Yes, Jesus. There are fakes and we must find a way to authenticate it without taking it apart, which may be necessary. Meanwhile, remember you sent it to a church and you don't know if it even got there. When they ask you where you sent it, tell them it went to Assisi. We have people there. Also, you should know that eventually you may have to return it, or at least sell it."

"I would never sell it."

"Your father said you wouldn't. Alright, let's forget about this now. As long as you don't have the Crucifix, you're safe. Let's go."

Chiara took charge of the wheelchair and they both moved silently into the viewing room.

Then Chiara bent over and whispered in Don Carlo's ear. "I have a lot of questions about why my father left Sicily and my mother went ahead of him and some other questions."

Don Carlo grabbed the brake of the wheelchair and looked up at Chiara.

"I know if I say there is no use asking about the past you are going to, anyway. My memory is not as good as it used to be. Bruno knows and remembers everything. In fact, over the years, and against my advice, he has written everything in journals he has hidden away somewhere. He knows everything and what he may not remember he can read in his journals. He is the only person, besides your father, that I have complete trust in. I have decided that he is going to help us once and for all to find out if the Crucifix is the real thing. Whatever he tells you is the truth. I guess some things don't really matter anymore because the people involved are dead, but I wouldn't tell anyone, aside from your husband, anyway."

Chiara rolled him back into the viewing room.

Chapter 11
Sonny Genovesse—A Subtle Threat

The funeral director nervously walked over to Donny and quietly asked if he knew where Chiara was and Donny told him probably in the viewing room with his mother. When the funeral director saw Chiara, he motioned for her to come over to him.

"Excuse me for the intrusion, but can you and your husband meet me in my office?"

"Yes, of course."

Chiara wondered what he could want. She would tell him the Crucifix was safely stored. Chiara found Joseph, and they met the funeral director in his office.

"Please close the door and have a seat. The first thing is that Father Ludovico was held up at St. Mary's Hospital, but he will be here shortly. Also, tomorrow we are having a wake in the other chapel and it may cause a little confusion. I tell you this confidentially. It is a soldier and there may be people from Washington D.C. who will guard the doors. His wake is private and just for the family and it is first thing in the morning, so there shouldn't be any trouble by the time you get here, but I have to warn you.

Joseph interrupted the funeral director. "Why all the secrecy?"

"All I know is that he was killed in a place called Viet Nam."

"Yeah, I've heard of it. I think I read about it and Walter Cronkite interviewed some politician about it on the news. They said that President Kennedy was just helping the French fight the communists, but he wouldn't let it get out of hand. But that is what they said about Korea. I hope this is not the beginning of another Korean war."

Chiara looked shocked at Joseph and then at the funeral director, who wanted to reassure them.

"Well, I never heard of it and don't know what all the fuss is. Anyway, I was told this is the first casualty and warned that if reporters get wind of this, there may be a problem. If it goes into the afternoon, I have been guaranteed it will be over before you and your family come and they are going to take the coffin to an undisclosed cemetery."

The funeral director again assured Joseph and Chiara there should be no problem and Father Ludovico would arrive soon. Chiara was already anxious because of the business of the Crucifix and now a late priest. Chiara looked at her watch.

"I hope Father Ludovico gets here before people leave; it's getting late."

As soon as Chiara and Joseph left the funeral director's office, the phone rang.

"Conte's Funeral Home. James Conte speaking. Yes, I think he is still here. Who may I say is calling? Just a second. Let me write your name down. Ok...Sonny ...Spell your last name...Genovesse. You want to hold? Alright, give me a few minutes."

The funeral director hurried into the viewing room, looking for Donny Buonoforte. He spotted him talking to Joseph.

"Mr. Buonoforte. There is a call for you in my office. It's..."

Donny looked at Joseph. "It must be Marti's wife, calling from the hospital."

"No, Mr. Buonoforte. Here's his name." The funeral director handed Donny the paper he'd written the name on. Donny read it and handed it to Joseph.

"Wow, Donny, what does this mean?" asked Joseph.

"I don't know. Come with me."

They walked to the office, led by the funeral director. Line one on the phone was blinking and without hesitation, the funeral director pushed the button and picked up the phone.

"Yes. Mr. Genovesse. Here is Mr. Buonoforte." He handed the phone to Donny, who took it somewhat reluctantly.

"Yes. This is Donny Buonoforte."

"Mr. Buonoforte, forgive me for disturbing you at your father's wake, but under the circumstances, I think you will understand. I am at St. Mary's Hospital and Mrs. Bonatti said I could speak to you directly. Her husband has suffered a mild concussion but the doctors say he will be alright. Mrs. Bonatti said she thinks you witnessed the accident and asked me to speak to you about it directly," Sonny Genovesse began.

"Yes, I was there. I understand it was your mother."

"Yes, that is the reason I want to talk to you. I discussed the situation with Mrs. Bonatti and I will take care of all the hospital bills and any other expenses. She wants you to understand we are not going to take this any further, so I hope you are going to cooperate with us under the circumstances. Do I make myself clear?"

Donny was shaking because he knew exactly what was being asked of him. "Yes. I have no interest in doing anything about this."

"I hope that is the case. It was very snowy and hard to see. Perhaps you made a mistake and didn't see what you thought you saw."

Donny covered the phone receiver and whispered to Joseph. "I'm being told I didn't see what I saw. It's a threat."

"Yes, Mr. Genovesse. Perhaps you are right."

"That's very good to hear. The officers said you would be cooperative."

Donny looked directly at Joseph. "As I said, I have no interest in discussing this with anyone and..."

Genovesse interrupted, "I understand that, but some reporters are already trying to make a story out of nothing and they already approached the officers who were there. They told the reporters there was nothing to discuss. I have your address and my mother will be sending a gift to show our appreciation."

Donny held his hand over the receiver again and whispered to Joseph. "Christ. He already knows where we live."

"Thank you," Mr. Genovesse said, "and if there is anything I can assist you with in the future, please don't hesitate to contact me. I had one of my assistants drop off a card at your parent's mailbox. If there is anything we can do for your mother, please have her contact me. Again, I am sorry to disturb you at your time of loss."

Mr. Genovesse didn't wait for Donny to say goodbye and hung up the phone. Joseph could see by the look on Donny's face that he was very nervous, to the point of being frightened.

"Well, Donny. What did he say?" Joseph asked.

"Well, he didn't say goodbye and just hung up before I could even say anything else. He told me in so many words to forget what I saw; his mother hitting Marti. He said Marti's wife wanted him to call me and that he is paying all the expenses for Marti, who, thank God, sounds like he is ok."

"Did he threaten you?"

"I don't know. He is sending a gift to my house and one of his assistants is putting a card in my mother's mailbox. I'm supposed to cooperate. I guess that means forget what I saw."

"Did he say how Marti is?" Joseph asked.

"He said the doctors said Marti suffered a mild concussion and will be alright. He is paying all the bills."

"As long as Marti is ok. You look shook up," Joseph said.

A few moments after they left the office, the phone rang again. The funeral director answered, then quickly went after Donny.

"Mr. Buonoforte."

At first, Donny didn't hear the funeral director who had to catch up to him. "Mr. Buonoforte, there is another call. It's Mrs. Bonatti."

Donny looked at Joseph.

"Shit. Donny, if was bad news Maggie wouldn't be calling you. Let's see what's going on."

Again, the funeral director led them into his office and left. Donny looked down at the flashing button on the phone and was hesitant. Joseph poked Donny in the arm.

"Well? You gonna pick up the phone?"

Donny pressed the flashing button on the phone. "Hello, Maggie?"

"Hi, Donny. Sorry to bother you, but Marti wanted me to call you right away."

"Jeez. How is he doin?"

"He has a huge headache, but he seems ok. He thought he was being funny because when he woke up, he made believe he didn't know any of us and scared the hell out of us. Sick idiot."

"Sounds like Marti. He must be ok."

"The only thing is, the doctors are concerned about his brain swelling more. They need to watch him."

"What do they do then?"

"I don't remember what the doctor said and at this point, I can't even think about it until it happens. Did Sonny Genovesse call you?"

"Yes, he called me."

"Well, he has some pull in the hospital and we have a private room in a private wing and a twenty-four-hour private nurse."

"Wow, he doesn't want anything happening to your husband."

"Sonny doesn't want anything happening to *his* mother if Marti dies. He met with the finance department and is paying for everything, including specialists if needed. He is even going to pay for a nurse and any other expenses when Marti comes home."

"Wow...Seems he's really nervous."

"Donny, there's another thing. I need some advice. I'm here with our kids and the head nurse pulled me aside and said my two brothers-in-law are downstairs in the main reception area and want to see Marti. I don't want to upset my husband, so I don't know what to tell them. I don't need this right now."

"Well, Maggie they are his brothers."

"Brothers! The only family ties they share are coming from the same womb. Other than that..."

"Then, say he is still not fully conscious and they can call you."

"No...I think I am going to see them. Did Genovesse tell you that you didn't see what you thought you saw?"

"Oh yeah. As long as he is taking care of you guys, what else can I say to him?"

"You're right. I really hope we don't hear from him. I'll keep you posted about Marti."

"Ok, Maggie. Whatever you need, just call."

"Thanks, Donny."

Donny hung up the phone and looked at his watch. Joseph was waiting to hear what Maggie had to say.

"Well?"

"Maggie is some woman. I'll tell you what she said while we walk. Let me just say first, his wife is some woman. She's a typical cop's wife. Tough as nails."

Chapter 12
A Woman to Reckon With

Maggie Bonatti realized early when marrying a cop that she had to be tough. When they had their first child and then their second, she had to be both mother and father. Her husband's work hours were erratic, and she had to live with the worry that the doorbell would ring and two officers would be at the door to tell her the bad news about her husband. Aside from being a beautiful woman, she was smart. Realizing that someday she may have to be the sole breadwinner, she went back to school and earned a degree in psychology and counseling. Maggie got a part-time job at the local high school as a counselor. She rarely wanted to discuss Marti's cases unless he needed advice using her education in psychology when he was trying to figure out a suspect or crime situation. Both appalled and fascinated by the crimes being committed made her even more anxious about Marti's job. Ironically, now that he was retired, would she be on her own after all the years of worrying, with him dying by getting hit in a parking lot by a gangster's mother?

Maggie went to the nurses' station to talk to the head nurse, who had told her about her brothers-in-law waiting in the lobby.

"Excuse me. Is there an area up here where I can have a place to talk to my brothers-in-law? A quiet and private place?"

"Oh, yes. At the end of the hall, there is an empty meeting room. It has chairs and a table. Would you like me to have your brothers-in-law meet you there?" asked the head nurse.

"Oh, that would be perfect. Thank you," Maggie replied.

"Mrs. Bonatti, why don't you stay with your family? I will get them and tell you when they are here."

"Would you do that? I would appreciate it so much."

"Not at all. Besides, my father is a retired detective, and he knows of your husband. He told me he's a great guy and I should do whatever I can to help him and his family."

Maggie teared up. There were many times people remarked on what a great guy her husband was, but it was not until now that she fully appreciated what they said. It was also a reminder of how much she loved him.

About ten minutes later, the head nurse signaled to Maggie that her brothers-in-law were in the meeting room. Marti was sleeping, as were her kids, in chairs next to the bed. Her son was holding his father's hand on one side of the bed and his daughter was holding his hand on the other side. As Maggie left the room, she looked back at the sight of the three of them and it made her choke up. The sight of them fueled her anger even more regarding her brothers-in-law, and now she would say what she had wanted to say for years without holding back. Her only regret was that their respective wives weren't with them, especially Vic's wife.

Vic and Joey heard the click of Maggie's high heels getting louder as she approached the meeting room, and they looked at each other in anticipation or nervousness. They knew this would not be an amicable meeting. They always were intimidated by Maggie. She was a strong woman, like their mother. Maggie slowly opened the glass waiting room door. Vic and Joey got up from their seats and walked toward her. She put up her hand, and they stopped in their tracks. At first, she spoke barely above a whisper to throw them off because she knew they would expect her to come in with guns blazing.

"Why are you both here?"

Vic meekly spoke first. "I saw he was hurt and we wanted to see if he was ok."

Maggie walked a little closer to them. "Who is *he?* You can't even say your brother's name?"

There was no response.

"I will ask you again. Why are you here?" Maggie's voice was still low and controlled.

Vic and Joey looked at each other, confused, which is exactly what Maggie wanted. Now Joey spoke up. "He's our brother."

Maggie let out a big laugh and replied in her normal boisterous tone. "Are you kidding me? *Your brother!*"

Now it was Vic's turn to answer her, and he did so with an attitude. "Yeah. He's our brother. After all, blood is thicker than water."

"Ha! Are you fucking kidding me? Well, so is sewage thicker than blood. The only thing you have in common is you all came out of the same womb. That's it. You're both jealous, resentful, and begrudging assholes. No matter what Marti has done for you and helped you and your families, you treat him like shit."

They were both silent.

"If Marti wants to see you, that's up to him, *boys*. And Vic, I put the blame on you for this. You..."

Vic stepped forward. "Wait one minute. That is not fair."

"Vic. Tell me what's fair. Are you two assholes fair? When your father was dying, where were you? When your mother was sick, where were you? I know where, and it wasn't with your father or mother. Was that fair?"

Then she walked over to Joey, almost nose to nose. "And you. You are the most ungrateful asshole I have ever met. You are a text book narcissist, one of the worst, and, as a psychologist, I've treated a lot of them. Self-centered, resentful, judging, gossiping, and then you even lie so you can turn people against each other."

Maggie was amazed that neither Vic nor Joey gave her any argument. She turned around and walked to the door. Then she stopped and looked at them again. "If Marti wants to see you, I'll be the one who will call you. But be aware, I will do everything to dissuade him."

As she walked out of the room, she raised her right hand and shook her index finger. "Watch your asses, boys. Karma's a bitch."

Vic and Joey looked at each other and sat down. For a few minutes, there was silence until Vic broke it. "Joey, what's a narcissist?"

"Just shut the fuck up."

Maggie returned to the hospital room and was happy to see Marti awake, but groggy. He looked at her and asked her where she had been.

"Just taking care of some nonsense. Nothing to worry about. Has the doctor been in to see you?"

The kids and Marti shook their heads no. Maggie kissed Marti on the forward and messed up his hair, which always pissed him off. Not this time. He grabbed her hand and tears fell from his eyes.

Chapter 13
Gianni Rudolfo Genco Russo

Donny and Joseph were glad to have talked to Maggie and found out that Marti was conscious. Joseph looked at his watch. "By the way, when is that priest getting here?"

"Let's go ask the funeral director to find out what is going on with Father Ludovico," said Donny.

Joseph saw the funeral director and waved him over to where they were standing. Joseph had heard the priest's name before but didn't know anything about him.

"Donny, how do you know Father Ludovico? I've heard his name before a few times."

"Long story," said Donny.

"Another one. Don't you people know any *short stories*?!" Joseph exclaimed.

~

Father Ludovico's name before he became a Catholic Priest was Gianni Rudolfo Genco Russo. He was born on February 19, 1926 in Palermo, Sicily. After his father died when he was sixteen, his mother sent him to Rome to a private school to study to become a lawyer, using his father's inheritance, as his father had planned when Gianni was growing up. For Gianni to agree to study law, he would only go to Rome if he was also able to study Italian art history. While studying, he often attended

Mass at the Vatican and became friends with some of the Swiss Guards. He would go on holiday with them, skiing in the Dolomites. He also spent his free time studying all the artifacts in the Vatican Museum.

During the summer months, he worked at one of the elite luxury hotels in the world: La Villa D'este, on Lake Como, Italy. La Villa D'este was built in the 16th century by Cardinal Tolomeo Gallio in 1568 as his residence. It was a time when the Catholic Church had not only all the power but all the money as well. Private ownership changed several times over the centuries, becoming a hotel around 1873 and then a retreat for rich Victorians. It has since been maintained as a luxury destination for the "rich and famous."

Gianni first worked at the hotel carrying luggage and providing "almost anything the patrons requested," as he was often instructed to do. However, he refused to comply with any "requests" that were not typical hotel services, regardless of any handsome tip. This would sometimes be difficult considering his thick dirty blond hair and deep blue eyes, unusual for an Italian, and his natural rugged build. A high work ethic inherited from his mother was another of his traits. He was fluent in French, German, and English and had a quick-thinking wit. Especially attentive to children, he was often requested as a babysitter but refused to watch any children in a guest's hotel room. Instead, to accommodate the guests needing a babysitting service, a small nursery was set up quickly next to the hotel's children's dining room. The room was decorated with wall paintings of German fairy tales, little tables and chairs, shelves filled with toys, and small cribs on wheels built to fit on the lifts so they could be rolled into a guest's room without disturbing the sleep of the child. The service became very popular. A small fee was charged to the guest who happily paid for the service, especially if Gianni was watching their child. Gianni was not paid extra but was often tipped handsomely.

When one of the assistant managers got wind of the lucrative tips by spying on Gianni getting paid by one of the guests, he told Gianni that he should pay him due to the assistant manager claiming that the hotel would use the funds to maintain the nursery. Gianni refused and immediately went to the hotel manager and threatened to quit. When the main hotel manager started asking the other staff members questions about the assistant manager, he found the assistant manager had been doing it to the other staff members and pocketing the money.

The assistant manager's behavior appalled Gianni, and he was the only one to come forward because the other staff members were afraid to lose their jobs if they said anything. When it looked like nothing was going to be done about the assistant manager's scam he quit in protest. With Gianni's reputation, he could walk into any other luxury hotel along the lake and get a job. When the hotel manager heard Gianni had quit, he fired the assistant manager and wanted to promote Gianni to the front desk as a hotel concierge. Gianni refused and instead applied for a concierge job at the beautiful Belle E'poque hotel, the Grand Hotel Tremezzo, across the lake from the small town of Bellagio. At first, the hotel had no interest in hiring Gianni because they already had a concierge, but the hotel manager from Villa D'este hearing that Gianni applied for the position contacted the hotel manager of the Grand Tremezzo and said if he didn't hire Gianni, he's a fool. He felt he owed that at least to Gianni.

In his new position, he attracted many rich and powerful clientele because of his good looks, charm, and job efficiency. With his salary as an assistant concierge and his handsome tips, he could save enough money to pay for a couple of weeks at the beginning of September to travel through Europe before returning to university. After a few summers he was offered a lucrative full-time management position at the Tremezzo, but kindly refused because he had plans.

Or at least his mother had plans for him to attend law school in Rome at the Sapienza University of Rome; a very reputable and prestigious school founded in 1303 by Pope Boniface VIII. While there, Gianni also studied Italian art history and, because of his interest in Vatican history and the Vatican Museum, he got a job during the school year on weekends as a guide for the Vatican Museum and the Sistine Chapel. Despite his busy schedule of attending class, studying, working on weekends at the Vatican Museum, and even some tutoring, his grades did not suffer. He found himself in the top one percent of his class.

After three years of law school, Gianni realized it was not his dream to be a lawyer, primarily because of his distaste for Italian law and also because he felt he wasn't ruthless enough to become a lawyer. Instead, perhaps because of exposure to the church, he chose to study Catholic Theology and subsequently decided to become a priest. The decision to leave law school was also encouraged in his mind by his mother's death, due to a stroke. Now, with his father and mother in "heaven," as he put it, he was free to determine his own future and undertake the *Rite of Ordination.*

When asked during his preliminary interview with some of the church representatives, Gianni said he wanted to be an "Instrument of God and serve the People." However, there seemed to be a small problem; his last name, Genco Russo. It was believed by some that he was a relative of the well-known Sicilian Mafia boss, Genco Russo.

Genco Russo was born in 1893 in Mussomeli, Sicily of very humble origins. He was a sly, semi-literate thug with excellent political connections. He was often photographed with bishops, bankers, civil servants, and politicians. As such, he was considered to be the arbiter of Mafia politics. When it was finally determined through some extensive research that Gianni had no connection to the Mafia boss, he was allowed to study to become a priest. However, some suspicions lingered, but people were afraid to ask. Even with his charming and warm personality, some feared him. The name of Genco Russo may have even worked to his advantage because there was much resentment and jealousy in the Vatican. Fear can be a good motivator to protect oneself. Some within the Vatican even thought he was sent under the guise of the Pope for the Pope's protection.

After a time, it didn't matter. He was a kind and attractive man who could charm people with his witty and warm personality. He was also highly intelligent and was well-liked as a result. Still, many were cautious, and many were covertly jealous.

There was possibly another reason, besides wanting to serve God. Gianni wanted to become a priest for a reason he never divulged to anyone. When he was around fifteen, his family took a trip to Assisi where young Gianni became enamored with St. Francis and the Stigmata, which are the same open wounds in Christ's hands and feet when Christ was crucified. Gianni saw for himself the cloth bandages with the blood that once wrapped St. Francis' hands and feet, which are displayed near St. Francis' remains in the Lower Basilica of the Basilica di Sant Francesco d'Assisi. From that time Gianni developed a deep sense of belief that never left him, even though he tried many times to push it to the back of his mind.

When Gianni was studying to become a priest, he often went to Assisi with another man who became Gianni's friend and mentor, Father Tommaso di Caltanisetta. Father Tommaso was much more of a skeptic than Gianni and almost scoffed at the idea of the Stigmata, even when he saw the bloody bandages. Despite Father Tommaso being an "incredulo Tommaso"—a doubting Thomas—as Gianni would refer to him, Gianni had a devout and unshakeable belief.

While in Assisi, Gianni also became interested in the man whose name Gianni would take as an inspiration: Father Ludovico di Cassoria. While Gianni was researching the Giotto frescos in the Basilica di Sant Francesco d'Assisi, he met some older nuns who knew of Ludovico's work in taking in abandoned children who lived in the streets of Naples and setting up orphanages and homes for the deaf and mute and the other good works that Father Ludovico dedicated himself to fulfill. He also set up an order of nuns and they all believed that Father Ludovico would someday become beatified and then be declared a saint by the Pope.

Gianni fell in love with Assisi and the tales of Ludovico and Saint Francis. After Gianni was ordained, he took the name of Ludovico instead of Francesco, as he had previously planned. He asked to serve in the Basilica di Sant Francesco d'Assisi.

While in Assisi, Father Ludovico worked part-time with Sister Bernadette at the Ludovico di Cassoria Center, which helped place abandoned children. Father Ludovico and Sister Bernadette were perfectly matched to work together. Their temperaments were the same, as was their devotion and love of serving God.

After a few years of working together, Sister Bernadette had become ill but refused medical care. It wasn't until she collapsed during Mass that she agreed to see a doctor. As feared, the prognosis was dismal; uterine cancer that had metastasized. There were no facilities in Assisi and a doctor suggested a new oncology clinic in Geneva, Switzerland that was conducting experimental treatments. That seemed to be the only hope. Gianni's father had left him a sizeable inheritance in an account in case of emergencies. He decided to use some of it to take Sister Bernadette to Geneva. However, train travel to Geneva would be too difficult, so he contacted Father Tommaso, who borrowed a car, and they took the long journey to Geneva, stopping along the way.

When they got to the clinic, the preliminary exam confirmed what the doctor in Assisi suspected, the cancer had spread. There were experimental chemotherapy treatments that were being tested, but they were very toxic and the side effects were difficult. Sister Bernadette refused the treatment against Father Ludovico's pleading with her to try it. The only thing to be done was to make Sister Bernadette as comfortable as possible for the time she had left.

For the next week, Father Tommaso and Father Ludovico kept a vigil until Sister Bernadette began to go in and out of consciousness. She had stopped eating, and the doctors said it would only be a short time until she passed. When it was Father Ludovico's turn to sit with Sister Bernadette, she asked him to hear her confession, but he didn't see the necessity.

"Sister, what on earth do you have to confess? You have been an angel on earth."

To his surprise, she took his hand, kissed it, and caressed it. Although she always called him Father, this time she called him by his baptized name.

"Gianni, I must confess...I must confess my love for you. Not as a nun loves a priest, but as a woman loves a man. In my life, I have never known such a man like you with a pure heart and pure soul and beauty. If there was any hint that you were thinking of leaving the priesthood, I would do all in my power to dissuade you of that thought; the church needs men like you. However, if you were set against staying; if you still insisted despite all my pleading for you to stay in the priesthood and instead you left; only then would I come to you if you would have me. So many times I cursed the church for not allowing us in the service of Jesus and God to take the Holy Sacrament of Marriage."

It was hard for her to talk, and Father Ludovico gently propped her up to take some sips of water. She continued, "My love for you has been a joy and a torture but for the love of God I have stayed steadfast that I would not allow my love and even lust for you to take you away from God and His service to the many you serve in his name. I accept my death with all my joy because I can now express the feelings I have kept in my bosom since I first saw you. Even the agony of love for you I do not regret for a moment."

Father Ludovico wept as Sister Bernadette poured out her feelings for him and held her in his arms when she finished. The next day, she fell into a coma. In her final moments, she opened her eyes for a second and he held her until the last breath left her body. He had to be torn from her. No other human had ever expressed their love for him in that way, and he knew it would never happen again.

Before they went to Geneva, Father Tommaso contacted the local bishop in Assisi to ask to have Sister Bernadette's body taken by train back to Assisi for a proper funeral and have her buried in the cemetery outside the Basilica. The bishop, knowing of Sister Bernadette's hard work and service to the church, quickly agreed. There was the financial expense, but Father Ludovico told the bishop he would pay all the expenses. The bishop insisted the church would take care of the expenses and that Father Ludovico would be reimbursed for any expenses he had already paid. Father Ludovico agreed, but said he would design and pay for her gravestone.

With the death of Sister Bernadette, something changed within Father Ludovico. It wasn't his faith. He had shed himself of his "innocent schoolboy" mentality. He found a new strength and toughness he had never felt before. Very soon, the situations he would be involved with would have him mustering up every bit of strength within his being.

Chapter 14
January 31, 1963, St. Mary's Hospital
Passaic, New Jersey

Father Ludovico parked his car behind St. Mary's hospital in the Chaplin's parking space. He looked at his watch and even though the hospital was only about fifteen minutes away from Conte's Funeral Home; he knew he was going to be a little late to give the blessing for Enzo Buonoforte and his family. He saw a man light up a cigarette and after all these years, he still craved one, even though he quit right after the war. He had avoided the fate of his mentor, Father Tommaso, who was in the hospital suffering from exhaustion, but he was also being tested for other problems; possible lung cancer. It had been a year since Father Ludovico had last seen Father Tommaso.

After the war, Father Ludovico came to the United States. Father Tommaso worked in Europe, helping to place orphaned children. They wrote to each other and sometimes would have a holiday call but the last time they saw each other was when Father Tommaso came to Sacred Heart Church to meet with Father Ludovico and place some Jewish and Christian children rescued from war-torn Italy. Father Tommaso didn't stay too long. He went back to Europe to locate refugee children with their parents.

They first worked together when anti-Semitism started in Italy in around 1938 when the Fascists banned Jewish children from attending schools; banned Jews from owning and operating a business; and not allowing Jews to attend or take part in anything of social relevance. Everything of value was taken from them and those who didn't flee Italy found themselves in a German concentration camp and most eventually died.

Father Ludovico tried to talk Father Tommaso into staying in the United States. Father Brunelli eventually left Sacred Heart and went to a different parish in Clifton. When Father Tommaso was at Sacred Heart Church, he explained his plans to Father Ludovico and Father Ludovico knew that Father Tommaso had a higher calling.

Father Ludovico stopped at the visitors' desk of the hospital and was given the room number and directions. When he got to the room, three nuns were sitting outside the room praying the rosary. He knew one nun, and he was introduced to the other two.

"Hello Sister Margaret, it is really good to see you again. Where are you assigned to now?

"We're in Ho-Ho-Kus. A beautiful church and convent. We teach at St. Anne's school in Fair Lawn. Father, I would like to introduce you to Sister Tommasina and Sister Sarah."

"Why, it's wonderful to meet you, sisters."

All three nuns looked at each other and giggled like young girls usually do.

Sister Tomassina put her hand out to shake Father's hand. "Father, we have met you before."

The two nuns again giggled. Father Ludovico shook Sister's hand and looked puzzled, trying to place the two nuns.

"I'm sorry sisters, I just can't recall."

"Oh, Father, it was years ago when we took a joy ride on a Red Cross bus!"

Father Ludovico looked even more confused.

Then Sister Margaret explained. "Father, Sister Tommasina and Sister Sarah were among the children you smuggled out of Italy and into Switzerland."

Father Ludovico seemed in shock. "Really?! Dear Lord. And you became Catholic nuns!"

Sister Tommasina explained. "Yes. Since it was you as a priest who saved us all, we wanted to show our gratitude for saving us by worshiping God and helping people in the way you do."

Then Sister Sarah spoke up. "Don't be too shocked, Father. It's the same business, just a different division!"

"That may be! It is wonderful to see you both. My heart is just so elated!"

Sister Sarah looked serious and reached out and held both of Father Ludovico's hands. "Father, we knew what you and Father Tommaso had to do to save us. We pray every day to God to thank Him for giving you both the strength to do what you had to do to save our lives."

Father Ludovico tried nonchalantly to take his hankerchief and wipe a tear from his eye. For so long, he had tried to block out of his mind what had happened in Italy years ago. Sometimes he had nightmares about it but knew in his heart-of-hearts that by saving those children he did the right thing...even if it meant committing murder.

Chapter 15
Italy, 1945. A road along Lago Lugano, toward the Swiss border.

After Sister Bernadette's funeral in Assisi, Father Ludovico decided not to stay in Assisi and instead once again joined Father Tommaso to work in Rome at the Vatican. By this time, Il Duce, Benito Mussolini, and I Fascisti were in power and were creating an alliance with Adolf Hitler. Many feared that it was an alliance formed in hell, and it would turn out that they were right. The people who were the most frightened were the Jews. The richer Jews got out of Italy when they heard rumors of the concentration camps in Poland and Austria. But then there were the poorer Jews who lived in the Jewish Ghetto on the outskirts of Rome. Many Jewish parents were determined to get their children out of Rome to Switzerland or another place like Sweden or Denmark that would take them. They sold their jewelry and anything of value to get their children to a safe place. But how? That was the dilemma. It's not clear how Father Ludovico got involved in smuggling children out of Italy. He joked with Father Tommaso that he had wanted to serve God and his people, but didn't imagine smuggling children was a way to do it.

The war was starting and with the help of Father Tommaso and some other priests; they came up with a plan to smuggle the children into the Vatican and out of Italy. They would have to do it without the knowledge of the Pope who had been threatened by Mussolini's Black Shirts not to get involved in the "political environment," as it was referred to.

A Jewish intermediary provided the money needed to bribe officials and any other expenses to get the Jewish children to a "safe haven." Very little was known about many of the young children who were smuggled out of the country since nothing was put in writing until they were in a safe place. It was then they were given their names and identities only through the memories of those who were rescuing them. Everyone felt the children's survival was of paramount importance, the rest would have to be figured out later.

The children were given a drug that left them unable to talk and put them in an almost catatonic state to get them out of the country without them showing fear or answering questions. All the children were dressed as girls because of the boys having been circumcised, which was an easy way to identify Jewish males. If anyone asked for an explanation, they were told the children were suffering from the shock of the war and losing their parents and they were being taken to an orphanage in Assisi or some other made-up area. Sometimes a priest dressed up as a doctor accompanied them.

Some went overland in the dark of night to Lake Lugano, where they were then brought by boat or car to the Swiss side of the Lake. Once there, people would take them to a safe house where they would get clothes. Then they disappeared into the population in Switzerland and other countries that would accept them. One of the most important facts to help the children was that Father Ludovico, as well as Father Tomaso, had photographic memories. They studied the name and background of each child and passed the information to the people who accepted them, so they could be reunited with their families if their families survived. No one knows how many of the families were eventually reunited with their children.

After a couple of years of anguish smuggling the children, by July 1943, it was clear Italy was losing the war. Then in 1945, Mussolini was captured before he could make it to the Swiss border and was killed along with his mistress, Clara Petacci, by Italian partisans. They were taken to Milan and hung upside down for public revilement for the masses.

After that, Father Tommaso and Father Ludovico were on their last rescue mission from a safe house in Como. Someone had absconded a Red Cross bus that would fit about twelve children. A map was provided that would take them along Lake Lugano instead of the Dolomite mountains. They got as far as the foot of Lago di Garda when two German officers pulled ahead of the bus and blocked its path. The officers made Father Tommaso and Father Ludovico, who were dressed as Red Cross workers, get out of the bus. The officers wanted to question them and the children. The Nazi officers didn't care that the bus was traveling under the guise of the Red Cross. Both Father Ludovico and Father Tommaso fooled the officers by speaking in Italian that they didn't understand German, even though both priests spoke and understood German fluently. The younger officer went inside the bus and the older officer, in broken Italian, asked Father Tommaso to see his Red Cross papers authorizing the trip. Of course, there were no such papers, but Father Tommaso motioned that the papers were in a briefcase in the luggage compartment on the side of the bus and he would get them.

When the younger officer came out of the bus, he tried to ask Father Ludovico what was wrong with the children. Father Ludovico told him with great emotion in Italian and with hand motions that they were in shock because of the war, seeing their families killed or missing. They were taking them to a hospital in a small town on the Italian side of Lake Lugano. What little Italian the officer understood, he seemed to be satisfied with the answer until he could see the papers. The two Germans were growing suspicious and said they would have the priests take their pants off to see if they were really priests and not Jewish imposters. Father Tommaso, hiding on the side of the bus, heard what the officers were saying. Instead of the fictitious papers, Father Tommaso held a large tire iron he had hidden on the side of the bus waiting to see if the officers were going to either let them go or kill all of them; it would be the later. The younger officer asked the older officer what they should do.

"Just shoot the two men and drive the bus over the cliff."

"With the kids inside?"

"Why not? They're dirty Italian vermin."

The older officer stepped onto the bus and looked around. When he came out, he commented to the younger officer. "Did you notice the children are dressed in heavy coats in the summer?"

"Hmmm. Maybe they are hiding something in their coats?"

The older officer told the younger to take two of the children off the bus and if they resisted; shoot them. They laughed and looked at Father Ludovico, who also tried to laugh after hearing their plans. He hoped Father Tommaso was planning some kind of move to stop them. At that moment, Father Tommaso came around the front of the bus and hit the older officer on the side of the head so hard, he fell onto the younger officer, who realized what was happening and pulled out his gun. Father Ludovico grabbed the gun and Father Tommaso hit the younger officer over the head, which splattered blood all over the windshield and hood of the bus. Some of the children had woken up with the commotion and were looking out of the windows. Father Tommaso pulled the bodies of the officers away from the door of the bus and yelled to the children to sit back down. Then he took his shirt off and wiped the blood off the windshield and hood of the bus.

"Gianni, let's go into their truck and see if we can find a shirt and any papers or anything we can use. Also, I saw a couple of gas cans. We may need them."

They went to the truck, took out the gas cans, and found two satchels in the back seat. One satchel contained clothes. Father Tommaso took a clean undershirt and put it on. Then they opened the other satchel.

"Dear God! Look at this! It's filled with money, lire and dollars. Stacks of hundred-dollar bills. Look at these papers. It looks like they were escaping to Switzerland. These passports look like fake Swiss passports. Let's get out of here. There may be others with the same plan. Wait, wait, wait, open the trunk."

When they opened the trunk, they saw a stack of machine guns. Father Tommaso picked one up. "Maybe they were going to shoot their way into Switzerland. Take two of them. Who knows?"

"You know how to use it?"

"Yeah. Point it and pull the trigger."

Father Tommaso took the truck out of gear and turned the steering wheel all the way to the right. They loaded up the bus with the satchels and guns. Father Tommaso took the guns and the gas cans to the back of the bus and broke the back window with the butt of one gun.

"Tommaso! What are you doing?"

"Taking precautions. Come sit in the back and keep watch. We can't get around their truck. I'm gonna push it out of the way with the bus. Help me load their bodies into the truck."

A few of the children were upset and others were waking up, not realizing what was going on. Father Ludovico explained they would have to be quiet, grabbed some sandwiches out of a cooler, and handed them out. Father Tommaso slowly pushed the truck out of the way with the bus. Before they left, he took a map from the overhead visor to determine how far the border was. They drove for about a half hour around the lake until they rounded a corner and Father Tommaso slowed to a stop. Father Ludovico walked from the back of the bus.

"Tommaso, what is going on?"

"Look. It's a checkpoint with two of those small German cars back-to-back blocking the way. Make the kids hide under the seats, then you come up here."

"Where are the guards? Can you see them? Are they in the guard-house?"

"I don't know where they are, but in case anyone saw the truck and the dead officers off the road, and somehow called ahead, the guards may be watching for us and are hiding."

"What should we do?"

"Were gonna pray this bus is strong enough to crash through those two cars."

"Oh, dear God!"

"Help me get this rearview mirror off."

They grabbed the large rearview mirror and broke it off the bracket that was holding it.

"Ok. Now sit on the floor and hold it sideways so I can drive the car from the floor. Ok. That's good. Hold it there and don't look up," Father Tommaso said.

He put the car in second gear for more power, got it up to speed, sat on the floor, and steered. "Everybody hold on and stay on the floor," he shouted.

From outside, it looked like no one was on the bus or driving it.

"Gianni, hold the mirror steady. I see two guards coming out of the guardhouse. It looks like they are trying to figure out how the bus is being driven without a driver."

"Do they have guns?"

"No...Oh geez. One of the guards is blessing himself."

"He must be Italian. Do you think they will try to stop us?"

"If they try, they're going to feel what it's like to be run over by a bus."

One guard was waving his arms in front of the bus to stop. Father Tommaso pushed harder on the accelerator and everyone again. "Hold on tight everyone and don't get up no matter what!"

When the bus came close to the waving guard, he jumped out of the way. The bus crashed into the cars and flipped them over out of the way. A few seconds later, Father Tommaso rose from the floor, got into the driver's seat, shifted the bus into a higher gear, and sped away.

"Gianni, look back. What do you see?"

"They are just looking at us and yelling at each other. How far do you think we are from the border?"

"Look at the map. We should be passing the town of Montelago-San Gottardo. Then it will be about ten or twenty minutes to the border, I think."

"Oh, geez Tommaso. I see two trucks coming toward us."

"Is there any insignia on the trucks?"

"Wait. Oh yeah. Oh, yeah. Nazi flags on the front fenders."

"Here, steer. Let me go back there. Kids, stay down!"

Then Father Tommaso went to the back of the bus. He saw two trucks in pursuit of them. He took the two gas cans and poured half of the gas from one can out the back window, then threw the half-filled can and the full can out, too. When the trucks were almost up to the cans, he took the machine gun and shot the cans, which exploded in front of the first truck and the second truck swerved off the road into a ditch.

"Tommaso, what is going on?"

"Eh, just some Nazi road kill!!"

When they finally got to the meeting place in Lugano, they contacted another priest who took them to a small church where they stayed until dawn. Father Tommaso and Father Ludovico took turns keeping watch; armed with one of the machine guns. In the early morning, they made another contact at the Santa Maria degli Angeli Church where they met some nuns who took two cars and drove them into Einsiedeln Abbey, on the outskirts of Zurich. When they felt they were finally safe, Father Ludovico dictated the name and family of each child to two of the nuns they were staying with. Two documents were filled out; one for record-keeping at the abbey and one that went into the pocket of each respective child. Now in Switzerland, the children would be placed in churches and in the homes of those who would generously take them until, hopefully, one day they could be reunited with their families if they were found and still alive.

Father Ludovico and Father Tommaso stayed at the Abbey for a few days and heard that the Allies were in Italy. Then they heard on the radio that Mussolini and his mistress Clara Petacci were caught on the road by Lake Como and were taken to Milan. The next day, they heard they were both hung upside down and killed. With that news, there was both joy and sadness. All those who were killed and over what? The machinations of a few evil men. Everyone in the house kneeled and Father Ludovico led them in prayer.

Father Ludovico realized there was no way he could go back to Rome. There were about a dozen children who could not be placed. Father Ludovico wanted to get them out of Switzerland and take them to America, but how? Then he remembered the money bag they took out of the Germans' vehicle. It not only had money from different denominations, but it also had jewels and some very expensive-looking jewelry. They planned on taking the children by rail through France which was also liberated and then go on an American troopship or plane. As amazing as it was, all the contacts were made, and it was decided to take the children and Father Ludovico to a small church in Clifton, New Jersey; Sacred Heart Church. While working in Rome, Father Ludovico had become friends with one of the other priests and had kept in contact with him; Father Anthony Brunelli. Father Brunelli had relatives who emigrated in the late 1930s to America when they saw what was happening in Europe. At the insistence of his family, Father Brunelli also emigrated to New Jersey. When he got there, his relatives had gotten him a position at Sacred Heart Church. Father Ludovico, knowing this, contacted Father Brunelli who agreed to help in any way he could.

The children and Father Ludovico left Switzerland and made it to Paris, where they met at a rendezvous point and were placed on a troop ship headed to New York. To Father Ludovico's surprise, when they finally arrived at Sacred Heart Church, Father Tommaso was already there to greet them in the church rectory.

"How the hell Tommaso?"

Father Tommaso laughed. "When I got to Florence, I met up with some army guys from New Jersey whom I knew when I was staying in London and Florence. They got me and the kids on a plane ride to London and then back home."

"Was that legal?"

"With everything going on and all the confusion, who was gonna question a priest and eight kids?"

Father Ludovico looked around. "Thank God. Where are the children?"

"There in St. Joseph's orphanage in Englewood. The orphanage took them in and we gave some generous donations to build more rooms and renovations, hire teachers to teach English, and all the other essentials these kids need. They are going to hire some people to get them to a local synagogue for Jewish instructions if they want, and also try to connect them with their families.

"But how?"

"You remember that bag I put on the bus? You know, the jewelry and a nice stack of American greenbacks, so I helped myself...in the name of the Lord, of course!"

Father Ludovico laughed. "God led you to your destiny, and you fulfilled His plans. Can you see that?"

Father Tommaso's tone changed, and he became very serious. "Answer me this; why did he create a war?"

Father Ludovico glanced at the Cross on the wall of the rectory. "Tommaso. God didn't create it, men did. There has always been war."

Tommaso walked over to Father Ludovico. "Gianni, there will always be the evil few dominating over the multitudes. The question I have is, who is more responsible for the bloodshed and misery: the evil few or the multitudes that stand by and allow the bloodshed and misery?"

Chapter 16
"Tommaso, you don't need *me* to intercede between you and God."

While the sisters were talking to Father Ludovico, he looked at his watch. He knew he was going to be late for the wake. "How is Father Tommaso?"

"Peaceful most of the time. He refuses to take a sleeping pill until he sees you. He wants to have a clear head when you meet," said Sister Margaret.

"Thank you, sister. What have the doctors said about his condition?

"He is suffering from extreme exhaustion and they are doing some routine tests to make sure he didn't have a heart attack, but they don't think so. They also want to make sure his lungs are clear."

"Thank you, sisters. Let me go in and see the old goat!"

The sisters giggled, and Father Ludovico slowly opened the door. First not to wake or startle Father Tommaso, and second, his apprehension of having to see him laid up in a sickbed. Seeing his old friend lying there immediately saddened him. *How virile he once was. What a larger-than-life man,* he said to himself. He had lost some weight. His beautiful, full blonde hair was thinning, and he looked so small in the bed. Father Ludovico stood in the doorway and then heard Father Tommaso's voice.

"Gianni! What do the old Italians say? 'Maledice la vecchiaia! Curse old age.' Ah, Gianni. My dear friend, you came."

"Of course, you old goat! I am here, but I can only stay a bit for now.

I have to go to Conte's funeral home to say some prayers."

Father Tommaso made a face. "Eh. What's the point?"

Father Ludovico ignored the comment like he had many times before when Father Tommaso questioned God's motives and even if there was a God. They both had seen too much, and it was easy to lose one's faith when witnessing so much evil made possible by so few. Father Ludovico wanted to change the subject.

"You know that two of the nuns who are praying for you out there are the Jewish kids we smuggled out of Italy? Sister Tommosina and Sister Sarah."

"Yes. How blessed. It reasserts my faith that there is a God. Sometimes."

Father Ludovico did not want to get into a theological debate and changed the subject. "What have the doctors said about your condition?"

"Eh...doctors. They say I need a rest and they want to make sure I didn't have a heart attack. I have to quit smoking, which I was doing anyway. I need to get out of here."

"You will get out of here when they say you can get out of here. I have an idea. Let's plan a holiday together and just go to some beach and rest and talk about old times."

Father Tommaso smiled and reached for Father Ludovico's hand. "Gianni, you make the plans and I'll be there, but first do something for me."

"Of course.

"Hear my confession."

At first, Father Ludovico didn't know what to say. "Tommaso, you don't need *me* to intercede between you and God."

"I think I do. I never said anything before...Gianni, there are times I seriously lose my faith."

"What do you mean?"

"Lying here, one tends to review their life and I have bitterness in my heart and an anger at God. Seeing everything that happened in the war, all the innocent people killed and even having to kill the German Officers."

Father Ludovico took a chair from the corner of the room and sat close to Father Tommaso. "Everything we did, we did for the survival of the children. It was either them or us and, most of all, the children. I wish we had killed more Germans."

Father Tommaso sat up with surprise. "Dear God! You have shed your little boy ideals! Bravo, Gianni!

"Well, we've been through a lot and we've seen a lot. I pray for those two Germans, but I won't regret what happened."

Father Tommaso sat back and stared at the ceiling. "My confession is because for a time I lost my faith and when I said Mass, sometimes I would look up and simply see a man on a cross. I still feel I have to confess and ask for forgiveness."

"Ah, Tommaso. I think of those dark times, but I am happy for the lives we saved despite killing those Nazis."

Father Tommaso just nodded and sat up. "After we go on our holiday and I'm strong again, I'm going back to Italy. Things are still a mess there and I promised Lady Madeline that I would come back. After I left her, she started working as a spy for the *partigiani*, the Italian resistance who helped her smuggle many Jewish children from Florence through her villa outside of the city. She hid them in tunnels until they were taken on fishing boats to Sardinia or some of the small islands around Sicily or wherever they could find a safe harbor."

Father Ludovico was familiar with who Lady Madeline was from letters from Father Tommaso.

"Have you heard from Lady Madeline since the end of the war? You had written to me that she was cut off from her husband in London and had to sell all her jewelry and some artwork to bribe officials and fishermen to take the children to safety. Are some of the children still stuck in Sardinia and the other small islands waiting to get rescued?"

Father Ludovico had been a little suspicious of Father Tommaso's relationship with Lady Madeline because Father Tommaso, before becoming a priest, was a "real ladies' man." He is over six feet tall with a very athletic physique from playing so many sports. The answer to why he became a priest would depend on who asked him.

He would sometimes say he heard the voice of God or some outrageous thing he could think of at the time. The *real story* was that when he and his brother Arturo were on holiday and were sailing in Naples, a storm with gale-force winds suddenly came upon them. The storm was so vicious it capsized the boat, but both of them held desperately onto the boat. Tommaso, in fear his brother would die, promised God that if he saved his brother, he would serve God for the rest of his life. Both men held onto the capsized boat and after a time, the storm let up and they got to a small island where they pulled the boat onto the beach. The boat was too damaged to sail. They found some people who lived on the island who gave them food and shelter until his family sent a rescue team to bring them back to Naples, where they were duly scolded. Tommaso told his parents of his promise and through some contacts, he was able to study in Rome and become a priest. He was assigned to a small church in Trastevere, the oldest area in Rome; Basilica of Our Lady of Trastevere.

Father Tommaso, while studying for the priesthood, took classes in Italian art and then taught part-time. He often traveled to Florence to take a few honor students on field trips to the Uffizi and other museums like The Academia to see Michelangelo's David. On one trip to The Academia with a few art students, Father Tommaso saw a beautiful woman at an easel sketching the sculpture of David: Lady Madeline Spencer Churchill, a cousin to the English politician Winston Spencer Churchill. When their eyes met, there was an instant attraction. However, when Lady Madeline noticed Father Tommaso's priest's collar, she tried to ignore him, but to no avail. Father Tommaso walked over to her to look at her sketch.

"That's a great likeness. Make sure you make all the proportions correct, though."

They both looked over at the statue and she knew exactly what he was talking about and they laughed. They struck up a conversation and when Father Tommaso's students finished looking through the museum, Lady Madeline invited the group to her villa outside of Florence for luncheon. The luncheon lasted for hours, with much talking about art and her gardens and just laughing. Lady Madeline swore to herself that she would not fall in love with a Catholic Priest, but before they left, Lady Madeline discussed her interest over the years in converting from being a protestant to a Catholic. She asked Father Tommaso for his advice and possible instruction.

"I love all the 'pomp and circumstance' of the Catholic Mass and the beautiful churches."

"Well, Lady Madeline, there is more to the Catholic religion besides 'pomp and circumstance' and architecture."

"Father, what I mean is that I feel so inspired and spiritual when I enter a Catholic Church and stay for mass. To me, it is so much more inspiring and spiritually lifting than our very dry protestant religion."

"Well, if you really are interested, let's begin with what you call the 'pomp and circumstance' and we can discuss the religious significance."

"That sounds wonderful. When can we begin?"

Of course, they both knew it was an excuse to see each other again. Lady Madeline invited the group back in two days for luncheon again and a swim in her pool. The villa was magnificent, with rare art and sculptures throughout the property. She explained to Father Tommaso that some sculptures had been illegally taken from Pompeii and were already installed when she and her late husband, Lord Westmont-Simmons, had purchased the villa. She also said when she sold the house, the statues would be returned.

Father Tommaso was surprised to hear her husband's name was different from hers.

"When my husband passed away, I took back my maiden name. I never really liked to be referred to as Lady Westmount-Simmons. My husband's family, I later found out, had less than a sterling reputation, which I'd rather not discuss."

Father Tommaso honored her request and didn't take the matter further.

As it turned out, Lady Madeline never became a Catholic, and Father Tommaso never divulged the nature of their relationship, but Lady Madeline made it clear from the start that she would never get between a man and his religion. Until the war began, they kept in touch and he visited as much as he could without any art students. When war did break-out, Lady Madeline refused to leave Florence and was fortunate to have an older neighbor, Sir Jonathon Dearwood-Smith. They became close friends because of their common interest in art. His villa was also filled with rare art and he hired a small army to protect the house and paid a lot of Italian officials and later Germans to not touch his property or Lady Madeline's villa.

Lady Madeline's villa was much older than her neighbors and had many hidden passages and tunnels to make a fast escape when the prior owners were being pursued because of art smuggling.

As Father Tommaso was explaining his experiences with Lady Madeline, he was tearing up and Father Ludovico could see that Father Tommaso had deep feelings for her.

"So, then, what happened to her?"

"I lost all contact with Lady Madeline at the end of the war and I feared the worst. When I finally returned to Florence and Lady Madeline's villa, she was gone and the villa had been ransacked. The once pristine gardens were overgrown and the beautiful pool that could have been in an emperor's villa was green and home to hundreds of frogs and bugs. Her neighbor was also gone, but his villa seemed like it was not touched and was now owned by a rich American. When I asked the new owners about Lady Madeline, the man said he had only heard she left with her small daughter and went back to England and I was dumbstruck that she had a daughter."

Father Ludovico gave Father Tommaso a look.

"Hey! Don't look at me. Even if I wanted to, it was 'hands and everything else off limits.' At that point, I left Florence and went back to Rome where there were more refugee children. There was confusion with letters that were coming in sporadically from parents or relatives who were now looking for their children that gave a name and description of a refugee child. Some families where the children were placed now refused to let the children go. Some children had been very small and now, years later, they had forgotten about their own parents and refused to be taken from their new homes. Another sad casualty of the war. We never forced any of the kids who were placed to leave, especially after one of the men who took in a couple of children met me with a shotgun. He said he would do anything to keep his children, and he wasn't kidding."

Father Ludovico nodded. "I guess if I were in their position, I would feel the same way."

For a few moments, there was an awkward silence. "Tommaso, meeting Sister Sarah and Sister Tommasino brought me back to what we did, what we had to do to save them. I hope in God's eyes he sees it the same way."

Father Tommaso lay back and stared at the ceiling. "There isn't a day that goes by that I don't think about what we had to do to save those children. That is why sometimes I have doubts about my faith and need forgiveness."

Father Ludovico wasn't sure how to respond. "If you no longer believe in our Lord, why are you confessing? I know you are just bitter, my friend, and I can't blame you."

Father Ludovico again looked at his watch. "Tommaso, I have to leave for the funeral home. I am late already. I will be back tomorrow, I promise. Mrs. Lourdes cleaned your room at the rectory, so behave and try to get out of here."

"Gianni, before you leave, can you tell those nuns to get lost? Last night it was dark in here, the door opened, and I saw these three black figures walk in. It looked like a trio of death angels. They scared the shit out of me and I chased them away."

"We rescued the two of them. You helped rescue them!! That is God's way of honoring your selflessness and goodness."

"I know, but it just reminds me of all the children who died that we couldn't save."

"Ok. Ok. I will tell them not to come in. They are praying for your soul, and it sounds like you need it."

They both started laughing, and Father Tommaso had a coughing fit. Father Ludovico went for the nurse.

"Gianni, GIANNI! It's ok. It will pass. See. I'm ok. Come back."

Father Ludovico went back to the bed and Father Tommaso calmed down.

"Are you alright?"

Father Tommaso nodded his head.

"Ok, Tommaso. Now, let's pray."

After some prayers, a nurse came in and saw that Father Tommaso was already falling asleep. Father Ludovico whispered to the nurse. "How is really doing?"

"Well, he is holding his own. Just get him to relax and absolutely stop the smoking."

Father Ludovico acknowledged what she said, but he knew Father Tommaso. "That may be harder than it sounds. But we will do our best. Thank you."

The nurse left, and Father Tommaso asked Father Ludovico when he could return.

"I have to see. Tomorrow, I have a service at the same funeral parlor. It's a private wake, so it should not take long. A lot of security."

"Gianni, why is that?"

"What I understand is that it's a soldier who was killed in some place called Viet Nam. It seems we're getting involved is something else that I hope does not turn into a Korean situation."

Father Tommaso rolled his eyes. "Oh, we will. Jesus save us...we will again. Are you leaving or what?"

"Don't worry Tommaso, I'll be back."

"I'm not worried about that. It's starting all over again."

Tommaso was almost asleep when Father Ludovico got up to leave. He looked back and tears fell. He wiped his face, opened the door, and saw the three nuns were still sitting there; still praying and saying the rosary.

"How is father?"

"He is resting. He is not ready to meet the Lord quite yet. And besides, I don't think they want him right now!"

They all again giggled.

"By the way, he said he appreciates all your prayers and asks that you please continue your kind efforts and maybe sit with him."

"Oh, that is marvelous news, Father. Thank you, Father. We will sit with him when we are sure he is asleep."

"That's wonderful. And sit close to the bed so he can hear your prayers even if he is sleeping."

"Oh, we will, Father."

Father Ludovico smiled. *Good for him!* he said to himself, *He will need all the prayers he can get!*

As Father Ludovico was leaving, he turned to Sister Margaret. "If you or Father Tommaso need anything, call me at the parish office."

"Oh. That reminds me, Father. We have been so lost in our prayers. There was a man who was here yesterday. He couldn't see Father because he was having an x-ray or some other tests done. The man, I think his name was Sir Smythe, or something or other. You know those accents are hard to understand sometimes. He said he couldn't wait to see Father because he had a flight to England, but he said as sure as he got some more definite information, he would contact Father."

Sister went into the large pocket of her habit, took out a thick sealed envelope, and handed it to Father Ludovico. "Oh, he left this letter for Father, but I didn't want to give it to him because I didn't know what it was and if it would be upsetting. I knew you were coming to see him, so I thought I would talk to you about it. Thank goodness I remembered!"

Father Ludovico took the letter addressed to Father Tommaso, marked, "personal and confidential." It also had the name of a law firm in London near the Royal Courts of Justice. Father Ludovico was familiar with English law and history from studying law.

"I'll take care of this, Sister. Thank you. Don't mention this to Father Tommaso. I will explain everything to him at the right time."

"Of course, Father. Thank you."

"Goodbye, Sisters. God be with you."

"And you too, Father. Safe travels."

Father Ludovico smiled and nodded his head. He walked away, holding the letter. There was no debate about whether to open the envelope. He had already decided to open it and, if the information was necessary, to give it to Father Tommaso right away. If not, he would wait. He sat in the visitor's lobby, took the envelope, and carefully opened it. After he read the letter and scanned through the accompanying papers, he dropped his hand with the papers on his lap and his mouth fell open.

"Ahh. Oh, dear God, now what?"

He folded the papers, placed them back in the envelope, and put them in his jacket.

Chapter 17
"Great. Happy 50th Anniversary, Momma and Papa."

When Father Ludovico finally arrived at the funeral home, he had to park across the street because the parking lot was full. The funeral director saw him and quickly escorted him into the viewing room to where Anna and her children were.

Father Ludovico took Anna's hands and offered his sympathy. "Mrs. Buonoforte, my sincerest condolences."

Maria and Giusepina were sitting behind Anna. Maria whispered to Giusepina, "Do you remember Father Ludovico? He performed the marriage renewal ceremony for Papa and Momma at Sacred Heart for their fiftieth wedding anniversary."

"Yes. I also remember two things: the ceremony and all the "agita" over the anniversary party that was supposed to be a trip back to Sicily. That was a mistake not to let them go."

Maria stared straight ahead silently.

~

"Chiara, please. How do you know they even want to take a trip back to Sicily?" asked Rita.

Rita wasn't the only one who asked that question. Chiara had already heard it from a couple of her other brothers and sisters but didn't care.

"Of course, they want to go back. Momma would like to see her sister before she dies. She's talked about it so many times."

Rita nodded her head, and it seemed she was coming around to the idea.

"Chiara, did you talk to everybody else?"

Chiara was thinking as fast as she could to at least convince Rita to buy into the idea.

"Yeah. Maria, Jack, Donny, everyone. They just want to know what it's gonna cost. I think before we talk to Momma and Papa, we get all the info about the boat and getting them to Sicily from Rome or Naples or wherever the boat goes in Italy and then to Mussomeli. We can send a telegram to contact Momma's sister. If they have a place to stay, that will save on hotels. Maybe they can stay in Rome for a couple of days and see the Vatican. You said your husband has a friend who is a travel agent or books trips. Let's find out before we ask Momma and Papa cause if the others don't want to chip in, then Momma and Papa will be disappointed if they know ahead of time."

Rita looked agitated. "You better."

After their discussion, Rita's husband Dante met with his travel agent friend who gave them the itinerary and cost of the entire trip. He met with Chiara and Joseph and presented it to them and Rita before trying to convince the others.

"They would sail from New York on the Cristoforo Columbo and make port in Civitavecchia outside of Rome. They would stay in Rome a few nights, then take a ferry to Palermo and a bus, or maybe they could be picked up by one of your mother's nieces or nephews, who could take them into Mussomeli. Regardless, everything would be arranged for their transportation and safety. It would be at least three weeks long. It wouldn't cost that much if they sailed second class and stayed in a modest hotel in Rome before going to Sicily. Then spending a night in Rome coming back before sailing home. The trip also included a guide and someone who would help them with luggage and arrangements, which added to the cost, but I think is a good idea. Another thought would be...maybe Antonino and Maria go with them?"

When Dante first brought the trip itinerary and costs home and showed Rita, she said it would be hard to convince some people to chip in. Dante, like Chiara, really wanted Enzo and Anna to go after years of work and bringing up eight children. They deserved a trip back to Sicily. After Dante presented the trip and the cost, he told Rita what to do next.

"There is only one way to find out if everyone is going to go for this. Call your sisters and brothers and have them meet here to discuss the trip."

Both Rita and Chiara called everyone, and they got together at Rita and Dante's apartment. Dante went over the itinerary and no one had any questions until they asked about the price. Maria and Antonino were the first to ask the question.

"We sailed on the Raffaello and it wasn't cheap even though we went second class and we didn't go to Sicily and we were only there for two weeks. And it's not as easy as you think. There are sometimes rough sea days."

Dante was hearing the whispers and comments and before it got heated, he tried to intercede. "Well, ya know, they aren't getting any younger. This may be their last chance. It is a great anniversary present."

Jack was the next person to speak up. "Yeah, You're right. They aren't young and they both have health issues. What if something happens when they're there?"

Chiara knew there would be objections and knew who would object *and* she knew how to address the "so-called" concerns.

"We know they have health problems. Older people travel back and forth to Europe all the time, and Momma and Papa will have an escort when they get to Italy."

Jack didn't give Chiara a chance to continue. "And what do we do if something happens or if they die while they're there? Besides, we all already chip in every week to help them."

Chiara was now fuming. "What the hell does that have to do with this? And what *if* they do die?"

There were a couple of gasps. Rita spoke up. "Chiara!"

"I don't give a shit. Isn't it better to have them at least try? What are they doing here? *Waiting to die?* Let's give them something to live for now...something to look forward to, something to talk about for the rest of their lives. And if something happens to them, at least they went and did something instead of staying here, having us, well, some of us, come over every damn Friday night doing the same damn thing."

Maria asked, "What is it gonna cost?"

Dante went over the costs and there was silence, followed by everyone talking at the same time about who couldn't afford it. It was too difficult; it was a lot of money, blah, blah, blah.

Chiara whispered to Joseph. "This isn't going to happen. It's just about the money."

Then Margo spoke up, and everybody turned to her. "Excuse me. I think it's a great idea."

Chiara was pleasantly surprised and agreed.

Then Jack, who didn't obviously care what his wife said, made a suggestion. "What about just giving them an anniversary party? It will only cost a fraction of what the trip costs."

Chiara snapped back. "It's a totally different thing. Let's just see who wants to chip in. If you don't want to chip in, fine, ok?"

Maria said, "That's not fair..."

Chiara interrupted before she could continue. "That's bull...c'mon Maria, who are you kidding? You could afford it the most. You should give the most."

"How much money do you think we have? I am not going to chip in cause it's too dangerous. Let's just have a party and then..."

"Are you kidding?" Chiara shouted at Maria. "You don't have the money? All your husband talks about is his damn Bell and Howell stocks. Who the hell do we know who owns stocks? The only thing we have are Green Stamps!"

Dante, who was also losing his temper, especially when it came to Maria, made a suggestion. "Why don't you and Antonino go with her? That would save the cost of the escort."

There was an awkward silence until Maria said, "My health isn't the best, then I'd have to take care of Momma and Papa."

No one else spoke and then it was finally decided they would throw an anniversary party.

Chiara said nothing and silently helped Rita get the coffee ready. While in the kitchen, Dante went over to Chiara. "At least we tried. I wouldn't push it cause if anything happens, you'll never hear the end of it and how would you feel if something *did* happen?"

"Great. Happy 50th Anniversary Momma and Papa." Chiara paused for a second. "I think it's worth trying again; I'm not ready to give up. I'm going to talk to Maria and Antonino alone. This sounds terrible, but even if something happened to them, at least they had some kind of real vacation. It's better than going down to the shore during the summer and renting a house. Then who does all the cooking and cleaning? You know who doesn't."

Dante patted Chiara on the back and kissed her on her head. "Good luck. You're going to need it."

Chiara waited a couple of days to talk to Maria about putting up most of the money, but it went as Dante expected.

"What are you kidding? My husband and I want to retire. An anniversary party is good enough."

Chiara was seething but kept calm. "Maria, listen. This is the best thing we can give them. How about all the years they helped take care of your kids when you were starting up the restaurant and when Jamie had his accident? You forgot? This is something that they could really look forward to and enjoy before they die. They aren't getting any younger."

"Let me talk to Antonino. I still think it's too dangerous and hard for them to travel with Papa's leg and Momma's knees. I'll talk to you tomorrow."

Chiara tried one more suggestion. "I have an idea. Why don't you both go with them or maybe just you, Maria? You would have a great time."

"I will talk to Antonino and call you tomorrow."

Tomorrow came and went, and there was no call. Meanwhile, the idea had cooled with everyone else and Joseph told Chiara to let it go because it was just going to create animosity even if Maria and Antonino paid for most of it, and they would never go because that would cost them even more and then they would be responsible if anything happened. No one ever brought up the idea again and over the next couple of weeks, Maria avoided talking to Chiara. When they did finally get together, it was all about the anniversary party. Maria and Antonino offered to pay for the band. It seemed a way to alleviate any guilt and, most of all, "save face."

The Red Hook Inn in Emerson was reserved, and the band was booked: Johnny Marchetti and his orchestra. Almost more than the food, the music was extremely important, especially to Enzo.

Enzo and Anna decided they would renew their vows on Saturday, January 8, 1955, at Sacred Heart Church with a reception following. The guests added up to almost two hundred people. That number included Anna's sisters and brother from Buffalo, which was agreed to after some heated discussions. The problem was, who would put them up? But that was quickly solved by having Enzo volunteer his kids' homes. Enzo and Anna refused to cut anyone from the list and threatened to have the party called off. The final count was two hundred and twenty and finally, no one objected, especially when Margo insisted her immediate family be invited.

Chiara and Rita took Anna for her dress at Mrs. Donahue's small dress shop on Main Street. An Irish immigrant, before retiring and moving to Clifton to care for her ailing father, she started out as an assistant wardrobe mistress in Manhattan and designed costumes for Broadway producers like Florenz Ziegfeld, Oscar Hammerstein, Billy Rose, and many others. Mrs. Donahue's father was a bootlegger during prohibition selling from his big house on Knapp Avenue in Clifton. His connections went all the way to Broadway, which was a big help to his daughter. However, it was apparent she was talented, and she didn't need her father's help. She made it on her own.

During those years, Mrs. Donohue got married and her father's bootleg business thrived. The only mistake was that she married a man who worked for her father. After a couple of years of marriage, he was found dead floating in the Passaic River. No one but her father knew why and for a time his daughter even accused him of having something to do with it because he didn't like the way her husband treated her. It created a rift between them for a time, but then, when she realized she was better off without her husband, things went back to normal. No one ever found out what really happened to her husband, although rumors came out that Mrs. Donohue's husband was either cheating on her father or some of her father's customers on whom one didn't cheat.

The bootleg business thrived up to the end of Prohibition. For years, Mrs. Donohue's father was protected because many of the police force at the time were Irish. They turned a blind eye and protected him even against the competing Italian bootleggers. Instead of wasting all his money, her father invested heavily in the stock market. Like millions of other Americans, when the stock market crashed on October 29, 1929, he lost almost everything. He saw many of his friends and business associates ruined and even committing suicide.

He kept up his bootlegging business, but this time he had saved up enough money "under the mattress" and bought some houses and rented them out. When a tenant couldn't pay their rent, he gave them a job landscaping or doing another type of job so they didn't lose their dignity, and he never had to throw anyone out of their apartment.

But for his daughter, things were just as bad as they were for many others. After the stock market crash, many Broadway theaters closed. It was said that the banks owned more of the theaters than the producers. Mrs. Donohue moved back to Clifton to live with her father, who convinced her to get out of the house and open a dress shop that he would invest in. Businesses were closing and store rent was cheap. She could cater to the wealthy people who lived in Upper Montclair, Englewood Cliffs, and other affluent neighborhoods where people weren't as badly affected by the economy.

Once she started advertising as a former "Broadway dress designer to the Stars" and dropped some names, the business slowly took off. After her father died, she kept the business and just did the designing. She hired other seamstresses to make the dresses. Anna Buonoforte could say a famous Broadway designer designed her anniversary dress. She never did, but her daughter Maria made sure everyone knew it.

Enzo insisted that Robert Hall was good enough for his suit rather than Arnie's Men's Store on the corner of Main Street. With all the planning for the party, any discussion or hard feelings regarding the Sicily trip were quickly forgotten. It promised to be a great time for the Buonoforte family.

Chiara and Rita reminisced that the family was acting together like they did before their brother Pietro died. Pietro brought a lot of fun into the house and he adored Anna. Every day, before he went home from work, he would stop to see his mother and sometimes he brought her favorite dessert; a Charlotte Russe. A push-up, paper cup filled on the bottom with vanilla sponge cake, with a generous layer of whipped cream, and a cherry on top. After Pietro died, she would never eat another. As a surprise, a few months after Pietro's death, Enzo brought one home but when he gave it to her, she threw it on the floor and said, "Mai! Never!" and she left the room in tears.

For years Pietro's name was rarely, if ever, brought up. On his death anniversary March 1st, Anna would quietly sit in her chair and hold on to his prayer card and Enzo knew to leave her be. Enzo also mourned, but in his own way, by tending to Pietro's grave at Calvary Cemetery. He had bought the grave plots for himself, Pietro, Anna, and Pietro's wife. All their names had been written on the tombstone, but only Pietro's had the dates filled in. He often wondered when the other dates would be engraved underneath the names.

As with other parents, when a child dies, there can never be the same level of happiness ever again. On the rare occasions when Anna and Enzo spoke of Pietro, they tried to comfort themselves by saying how many families lost sons in the war. Some parents lost more than one son. Anna always remembered the movie that Chiara and Rita had taken her to at the Clifton theater, *The Fighting Sullivans.* In a way, Anna scolded herself for thinking that she lost only one son. The mother of the Sullivan boys lost all five in WWII. Through some tears, Anna told Enzo about the movie.

"I can't believe the parents lost all five of their sons in the war."

Enzo looked down and said, almost in a whisper, "All five sons killed on one ship. How could that happen? We only lost one."

Anna took the hankie from the inside of her apron pocket to wipe her tears and shook her head. "If only women ruled the world. Would they send their sons and daughters to war?"

Enzo stared at Anna for a moment and realized again how she and some other women could be so much smarter than men. They sat silent until Enzo gave her a little slap on her leg and pinched her cheek like he did when they were young.

"Ti amo bella."

"Anchio ti amo."

For the short time during the weeks of planning the anniversary party, the Buonofortes were enjoying themselves as a family again. When the day arrived, Anna and Enzo looked radiant. Enzo's blue suit was perfectly tailored with a crisp white shirt and a tie matching Anna's dress. Mrs. Donohue went beyond anything that was expected and people knew she spent much time herself working on the dress. She remembered designing a dress for the movie star Marie Dressler, who was a little bigger than Anna, but the dress suited Marie Dressler perfectly. Mrs. Donohue used the same pattern and tailored it for Anna. As she did for Marie Dressler, Mrs. Donohue suggested a light blue dress, with pearl accents, and just enough lace and layers of taffeta that it would not look dated or overdone, and everyone agreed the dress looked beautiful on Anna, whose hair, nails, and makeup just highlighted her radiant appearance.

When Enzo saw her, he clasped his hands together, simply saying, "che bella la regina." During the church ceremony, they acted like young lovers and enjoyed every minute. There was true family harmony. Many of the activities were documented in home movies and photographs that would be enjoyed by everyone on certain Friday nights when some of the Buonoforte family would get together at the East Clifton Avenue house. Enzo would be seen kissing Anna at the dais with their children seated on each side of them. Enzo took one of his cigarettes and put it in Anna's mouth, and since she never smoked, the family roared with laughter.

Before each course of the meal was served, Enzo would go into the kitchen and remembering his experiences working in Angelina Trattoria, wanted to make sure each course was served at the right temperature. Normally, instead of cooking the pasta to order, the caterer would take partially cooked pasta, put it in boiling water for a few minutes, and serve it that way. Enzo insisted the pasta and ravioli being served were cooked to order, instead of cooking it first and then warming it up to serve. He explained to the chef when discussing the menu and planning the party, to have more than one pot of water boiling and carefully timing the cooking of the pasta according to the number of quests, which would allow for all the pasta being served hot at the same time.

The cans of tomatoes were from the San Marzano region of Italy, outside of Naples, where the tomatoes are grown near Mount Vesuvius, which destroyed Pompeii and Herculaneum in 79 AD. Even the chicken and other meats would have to come from the butchers and produce stores that Enzo recommended. Enzo, who had gotten wind about the anniversary party instead of the trip, figured *I get the food that Anna and I want.*

After Enzo spoke to the chef and was pleased, he left and was called over to have the family picture taken. When the family got the pictures back, they teased Enzo, saying he looked so pleased with himself because of his involvement in the cooking of the food. He laughed and said that wasn't it. He told them Anna had her hand on his "backside" trying to pinch him and he was trying not to laugh.

The big surprise would come when Chiara's name was announced to sing the first dance for her parents. More than anyone, Enzo was so happy he tried as hard as he could not to let the tears fall from his eyes. Anna grabbed Enzo's hand and Chiara sang one of her favorite songs, *Peg of My Heart.* When she came to the lyrics, "...it's your Irish heart I'm after," she changed it to "It's your *Sicilian heart* I'm after," and the crowd went wild standing, clapping, and cheering. When she finally finished, everyone again stood, cheered, clapped, and shouted, "ancora, ancora, more, more." She sang one more song; the Italian, *Non Dementica.* The shouts and clapping were even longer and seemed to last forever. Even the band stood and the band leader whispered in her ear, "Where have you been all my life? What talent!"

Chiara laughed and said, "Yeah. Sure."

As she left the stage, she saw her brother Jack clapping, and she smiled. Before she walked past him, she whispered in his ear, "Marginal talent, eh? Bastardo!" He looked away, embarrassed and ashamed.

When Chiara was in the church choir, the choirmaster said that she should study singing. When she told her parents, Jack was there as well.

"Forget it. You should just get a job. Get married. You only have marginal talent and you don't know how hard show business is," Jack said.

Enzo yelled at Jack and told him to mind his business, but it was too late. Chiara was deflated. She kept singing with the choir but lost interest, especially after Pietro died.

After hearing Chiara sing, Anna and Enzo ran up to her, embraced her, and said that was the best present they could have ever gotten. Chiara looked back at the band smiling and her thoughts went to a lost love and a lost opportunity, but it was just for a moment. She caught a glimpse of Joseph, thought of her kids, and almost said out loud, "My life is so much better."

As the evening came to a close, Enzo became very melancholy by how many people came over to him and Anna and reminded both of them of the many kind things they had done over the years, by bringing food to some poor families around the holidays who were hard up. Also, leaving food in a basket on their doorstep, not wanting to embarrass any-one. But everyone always knew who it was and knew that Enzo was not keen on gratitude, but no one ever forgot. Some friends ridiculed Enzo, saying he would never get rich by giving food away. But Enzo would just laugh.

"You want to see my riches and my treasure, eh? You come to my house and see my family. That is *my* gold!"

Enzo's melancholy turned to sadness remembering how many people were missing or had died over the years, especially his Pietro.

When the evening finally came to a bitter-sweet end, Anna and Enzo wondered if they would ever again see many of the people who came to honor them. As for the Buonoforte children, the evening had them realize that Enzo and Anna would not live forever and the anniversary party, in a strange way, was a bitter reminder of that fact. The evening would be the climax of their life. But no one spoke of it openly. It was too hard to even consider, especially for Chiara. As they were leaving, Joseph took Chiara's arm to walk her out of the hall.

"Boy, everything turned out so great. Even the food wasn't that bad. Your parents had a really good time. And your singing! That was the best thing you could have done for them. You were really great."

Chiara looked straight ahead knowing that tonight her voice and singing were never better and even so, she would never sing in public again.

"Yeah, they had a really good time."

They walked to their car without a word and were silent on the drive home, neither wanting to admit the obvious. Anna and Enzo were in the autumn of their lives. They both wondered if Anna and Enzo had realized it, too. How could they not? Chiara would cope with the same thought and live in denial.

Chapter 18
"After your nonsense, including all of us, only sixty people showed up."

The second day of the wake was much the same as the first day. The realization that Enzo was gone sank in deeper, especially for Anna. Enzo had taken care of everything, not only taking care of the house and paying bills but keeping up with their friends. This was made evident by the people who came to pay their respects. Some people just knew Enzo through their store years ago, either through business dealings or things Enzo did for them during the hard times. Chiara remembered who some were because she was with Enzo when he would drop off food to many families when their husbands were out of work. Many of the charitable acts that Enzo did were told to Anna as the families personally paid their respects. Anna didn't know who many of these people were and in many cases was surprised because Enzo never told her about the things that he would do for the different families.

For the most part, the funeral services went pretty much as planned. Father Ludovico started with the visitation in the morning at the funeral home, then the Mass in Sacred Heart Church, and finally the arrival at Calvary Cemetery. The only event that created some confusion was the private wake for the soldier that was taking place the same day as the Buonoforte funeral.

Father Ludovico would need to finish with the Buonofortes and then rush back to the funeral home from the cemetery. Government people came in the morning to make sure everything was according to plan, which created a constant checking of rooms, talking on walkie-talkies, and Buonoforte cars trying to leave the parking lot with the government cars trying to come in. It seemed the goal of the government officials was to keep the unwanted press from coming into the funeral home. The soldier killed was the first casualty in Viet Nam and things were heating up as the United States became involved. The government wanted to keep a low profile for as long as possible until the government could come up with a plan they could share with the public.

The cemetery did a good job of clearing the snow. In a way, it was a distraction from the funeral, having to make their way to get a seat near the gravesite. There was such a crowd at the cemetery that many people had to stand. Anna sat in the first row with her children and respective spouses on either side or in a row behind her. As they were waiting for Father Ludovico, Chiara saw Dante get up and talk to a woman toward the back of the tent.

"Rita, who is that woman your husband is talking to?"

Rita seemed annoyed at Chiara bringing attention to her husband and the woman. "How should I know? Maybe someone he works with."

Chiara stared straight ahead. "Oh."

Father Ludovico arrived at the cemetery and gave a beautiful sermon and sendoff for Enzo. There were many tears, but mostly everyone, including Anna, was calm. After the cemetery, people arrived at Johnny's Bar and Grill for the repass. At first, it was Jack who was concerned about how many people would show up and the cost. Chiara had told Johnny to expect around seventy-five people, other than trying to count the family; it was hard to tell. Now it was Chiara who was concerned because there were a lot of people at the cemetery.

Johnny's was a popular place for parties and events because of the reasonable price and the home-style cooking. The meal started with a simple crudité of celery, carrots, and olives. This was followed by a cup of chicken soup, then meat and cheese ravioli from North Jersey Ravioli. The main course was hot roast beef and gravy, roast garlic chicken, mashed potatoes, and vegetables. The desserts were pastries from nearby

D'Anna's bakery, coffee, and tea. Except for the dessert, everything was served family style and as much as you could eat. Some people were annoyed that they couldn't take home a "doggie bag" of food. Johnny learned early on that people would order more than they could eat and take the rest home. Even though taking food home wasn't allowed, some of the women would take small containers or plastic bags and sneak the food into their purses. "After all, I can't eat my share and I'll just have it tonight for dinner," was their attitude.

As the last few people arrived at Johnny's, Father Ludovico came back from Conte's Funeral Home after the service for the American soldier. He said a few nice words about Enzo and the Buonoforte family and then said grace.

Chiara kept after Anna to eat. She said she wasn't hungry and just nibbled on some chicken. Chiara insisted to one of the servers that Anna be able to take her meal home, which was graciously allowed. Before they left Johnny's, the servers packed even more food for the family to take home. Jack came over to Chiara toward the end of the meal. Chiara anticipated what he was going to say and cut him off before he could begin.

"Look, Jack. After your nonsense, including all of us, only sixty people showed up."

Jack looked around the room as if to count the people. "How do you know that is the exact amount?"

"Because Momma and I just paid the bill, like I had been telling you, she would. As usual, they did a great job. Go look for your wife and kids."

Before Jack could say anything, Chiara walked away to sit next to her mother. Everyone began to leave and Anna dreaded them coming up to her to say goodbye. She just wanted to go home. Finally, she didn't wait for the last person to leave and she called out to Chiara to help get her up and take her home.

"Chiara, andiamo. I want to go home now."

Anna said it with such force that Chiara didn't argue with her to wait for the last person to say goodbye and leave. Anna didn't care if it seemed rude. She had just buried her husband and her future was in doubt.

Chapter 19
Paramus Nursing Home, Spring, 1966

Before unlocking the door to her office, Anna Avero reads the bronze plague hung there and gently moves her fingers across it.

Anna Avero

Nursing Home Administrator.

She wonders, under the circumstances, how long her name is going to remain on the door. She didn't know if she really wanted to juggle motherhood and a career. As she fumbles through her purse for her office key, she hears the phone ring and drops the key. As quickly as she can, she picks it up and nervously unlocks the door. She takes off her coat and throws it with her purse on the chair by the small glass conference table. A few seconds later, Mrs. Petersen walks in with a tray holding a cup of tea and a couple of pieces of dry toast. Mrs. Avero picks up the phone but whoever is calling has already hung up. Mrs. Petersen puts the teacup and saucer and the small plate with the dry toast on the desk.

"That must be your father-in-law again. He called three times this morning."

"Oh, good morning. I'm sorry I'm late. This damn morning sickness is getting worse."

"Here. Have some tea and toast. It always helped me with morning sickness."

"Thank you. You're an angel. Did my father-in-law say what he wanted?"

"Only to talk to you. He sounded somewhat anxious."

When Mrs. Avero found out she was pregnant, she promoted Mrs. Petersen from secretary and receptionist to assistant administrator, and she was thankful she did.

"That's just what I need, some tea. Thank you. I wonder what my father-in-law could want?"

"I'm sure he'll call back."

Mrs. Avero looked at her watch. "I have Mrs. Fonte on my schedule this morning. Did you confirm?"

"Yes, she will be here at 11:30 to speak to one of the staff psychologists and then speak to you."

"Let's have her sit with her mother for a few minutes before going into the dining room for lunch, so it is more comfortable. Maybe she can convince her mother to eat more. I am worried about her."

"You know, we have seen this transition before. When a new resident gets here, depression sets in and they just begin to fail. You're doing everything you can for Mrs. Buonoforte."

"Well, she is really family. My long-lost godmother. In the Catholic religion and especially in the Italian culture, a godmother is taken seriously; at least it used to be that way. Things change and not for the better sometimes."

At that moment the phone rings, and Mrs. Petersen, who is closest, picks it up. "Mrs. Avero's office, may I help you? Yes, she just got in."

She hands the phone to Mrs. Avero and mouths that it is her father-in-law. Mrs. Avero rolls her eyes and takes the phone. Before she can even say hello, her father-in-law speaks in a tapped down frantic tone.

"Anna, we're being sued."

Before Mrs. Avero has a chance to think about what she has just heard, he repeats in a more frantic tone. "Did you hear me? We're being sued!"

"Ok. Dad, I hear you. What are you talking about?"

"Oh. You finally heard me."

"Yes, I heard you. It won't be the first time. What the hell are you talking about?" Anna asks.

Mrs. Petersen hangs up Mrs. Avero's coat and purse and quietly walks out and closes the door.

"Do you remember a woman who came to you about placing her mother a few weeks ago?"

"I saw lots of women a few weeks ago who wanted to place their mother."

"*You* told me something about this one. A real pain in the ass. Does the name Fontanella ring a bell?"

Mrs. Avero thinks for a moment and then it hits her like a sledge-hammer.

"Oh, no! No, no! Not her!"

"Yes *her*. Mrs. Martino Fontanella of Upper Saddle River. Mrs. Lorileigh 'don't call me Lori,' Fontanella of Upper Saddle River, I stand corrected."

"Oh, my God...she's suing to get her mother in here?"

"Oh, no...she is suing the nursing home AND you! It seems it's no longer about her mother, but that's probably part of it."

"Me? Why? Because I told her that her mother isn't a candidate for a nursing home? We had her mother examined mentally and physically. I even spoke to her mother, and she *does not* belong in a nursing home or even *wants* to go into a nursing home!"

"Calm down. I may know that, and you may know that, *and* the old lady knows that, but Mrs. Fontanella of Upper Saddle River thinks differently and refuses to know that."

Mrs. Avero sits back in her desk chair and covers her eyes with her hand. "I don't care what she does; her mother is not getting in here as long as I'm in charge, otherwise I'll quit. She is trying to dump that poor woman because her mother is an inconvenience."

Anna's father-in-law, having shared the anxiety has calmed down. "Tell me again exactly what happened. I know we discussed it, but..."

"Yes, I discussed it when it happened. You and my husband were having a father and son drinking contest with Strega Martinis."

"Oh, yeah!"

"If your wife had been there...Shit...Oh, I'm sorry. I wasn't..."

"Don't be sorry. You're right. My wife would have been pissed off that her son was overdoing it and I was encouraging him. Then after you guys left, I would have been given a pillow and blanket with no explanation, the bedroom door slammed, and me in the doghouse for days. Ah...but making up would be wonderful..."

Mrs. Avero can hear the cracking in her father-in-law's voice and quickly changes the subject. "Well, initially Mrs. Fontanella brought her mother in, and as I told you, her mother was interviewed by our staff psychologist and had a thorough physical exam, which I made sure Mrs. Fontanella, or whatever her name is, paid for. I even interviewed her mother. This woman was not, and probably is still not, a candidate to be in a nursing home...nor did she want to be. She confided in me she thought her daughter didn't want her around after her grandchildren were grown. She helped raise them, but now her daughter makes her go in her room when she gets visitors and she doesn't need her anymore."

"So, then, what is the problem?"

"She came in to discuss the tests and she was so arrogant. Basically, I told her that her mother was not a candidate and that was it."

"That was it?"

"Well, I did tell her off."

"Yeah, well, that is one of the reasons she is suing us."

"I'm sorry. She had it coming the way she was treating her mother and I..."

"That may be true, but now we have a problem. I don't want this to turn into a P.R. nightmare."

"When were you served papers?"

"I haven't been served papers yet, but..."

Mrs. Avero cut him off. "Then why do you think we are being sued?"

"You know Pete Carbone?"

"Yes. I think my husband helped him get his son out of trouble or something."

"Yeah. A marijuana charge. Well, Pete was volunteering at the bar at the Italian Brotherhood of Bergen County and he overheard it."

"The Italian Brotherhood...Wait that sounds familiar. I read that somewhere..."

Her father-in-law cut her off. "Ok. This is the thing. Do you remember when Danny, your young resident, had one of his severe epileptic episodes the day she was there?"

"Yes, I do and I had a feeling it was not a good situation. I had Mrs. Petersen escort her out of the building."

"That's fine, but before Mrs. Fontanella left the building, she saw what happened and saw young Danny. She asked one of the staff why a young guy was there and one of your brilliant staff members said it was because his parents paid for some construction of the new wing and..."

"That's not true! Who the hell said that? I'll fire their butt right now!"

"Take it easy. It *is* true, but that was *before* we took over the nursing home from bankruptcy and saved it. We inherited Danny, and he needs to be there because he needs constant care. His parents are dead and he has no close relatives. We signed an agreement to accept him from the previous owners to keep him there when we took over. But that is beside the point. Danny is not the issue."

"Well, I'll quit and your problem will be solved. I don't know if I can or want to juggle being a mother and having a career."

"First, quitting will not solve the problem. She will still come after you and the nursing home." Her father-in-law ignored Anna's second comment. "We have Joe Russo in our firm who handles stuff like this to head this off."

"You are not thinking of settling because if..."

"Russo is a shark, and he knows exactly how to handle this."

"But who did Mr. Fontanella talk to about this? Who did Pete overhear this from?"

"Believe it or not, Danny's legal trustee is Art Dunatto. Art is friends with Martino Fontanella, who is married to..."

"Yeah, I get it, Mrs. Fontanella."

"No, not merely Mrs. Fontanella. Lorelei, not Lori Fontanella of Upper Saddle River."

"You keep saying that. What the hell do you mean 'not Lori'?"

"She does not like to be called Lori and she will correct anyone who calls her Lori, AND she wants everyone to know she is a big shot living in Upper Saddle River in a big house. Get it?"

"My God...So then, how did Art get involved?"

"Pete was on the side of the bar behind a small partition fixing a drink and he said he heard them talking. Martino was telling him about what happened at the nursing home and how pissed off his wife is and she is making his life miserable. Art told him he had a connection with the nursing home with Danny and he would handle the case 'pro bono' as a favor, and Martino should sue. Martino agreed."

"But wait. If he is Danny's legal guardian, isn't that a conflict of interest and he may harm the place where Danny is living?"

"We know. That is going to be part of the defense, but there is more to it. Pete said that Art is also Danny's benefactor upon Danny's death. Look at Danny's file. He is paying top dollar for private care which goes up with the cost of living every year. There is a lot of money in his account, but it is getting used up. And then there are the legal fees. I don't know if he's doing anything wrong except maybe charging huge fees. We are going to use 'conflict of interest' as leverage behind the scenes. If we can scare Art, then maybe the Fontanellas won't want to pay for another lawyer and they may forget about it."

"Yeah, but why would Art want to hurt the nursing home where his own client is getting great care?"

"Why? He's a scumbag. Art is old and Danny's young. We think Art doesn't want that money used up and this is a good excuse to get him out of our facility. Then he can put Danny in a cheaper place, probably try to sue us, and take the money for legal fees from Danny's estate at a high rate. When the money runs out, if Danny lives long enough, then Danny gets dumped on the state."

"What a bastard."

"Well, it isn't a 'fait accompli.' Russo has some excellent strategies and has already found some precedents. Not to change the subject, but changing the subject; how are you feeling? Still with the morning sickness?"

"Yes, but I can handle it. Your son is being really good about it because you know him; he gags at anything. Does he say anything about being a father?

"He is thrilled but we don't get to talk much because he is trying to get all his cases closed or handed over to one of the other associates when they go to court. He wants time off when you have the baby."

"Nicky said he is going crazy, and I told him to do what he has to do so he can take the time off."

"What are you going to do about the nursing home when you have the baby?"

"Well, I promoted Mrs. Petersen and I'm training her to take on more responsibility. I want to see how things work out. If we go to trial, I may even be gone on maternity leave. Like I said, and you ignored, I don't know if I want to be a mother and a career woman."

"I didn't ignore it. I chose not to respond because we need you. Besides, nothing will probably happen until after you have the baby. I understand there are more important cases on the docket that have a priority."

He changed the subject because he didn't want to think about the nursing home without his daughter-in-law running things. "We're going to fast-track this Fontanella lawsuit. I have the accountants figuring out if it is worth it just to settle as a Plan B. It would be foolish to rack up a lot of legal fees. We need to at least analyze the situation. We have a fiduciary responsibility to the other partners, but I want to fight this one."

"Yes, but they're also taking a risk they may lose if you go to trial."

"That is what we are calculating and Russo is going to weigh in on it, too. But for now, don't worry about it. By the way, Nicky said that your mother is flying in, when?"

"Next Monday. Nicky insists on picking her up at the airport. I think my mother likes him more than me and he is crazy about her. Guess it's the way she dotes on him. The first thing my mother will do is see if there's any wash that needs to be done and the second thing is she'll make your son her pineapple upside down cake. She already telephoned me with a shopping list," Anna says.

"That's what my wife used to make him all the time. I was lucky if I got a slice. I think Nicky misses his mother. She adored him without trying to spoil him, but she did. I think he misses her more than I do if that's possible. You know a mother and her son..."

"He doesn't really bring her up and if I do, he changes the subject."

"That's my son. He doesn't like to discuss his emotions too much. I want to see how he will be with the baby."

"I think he may surprise you. If a movie or song comes up that reminds him of his mother, he'll say something like, we always watched that movie or my mother loved this song."

"I'm glad he could spend so much time with her toward the end. I chose to spend more time at work picking up his slack so he could have more time with her. It's what she wanted, too. I just couldn't see her fade away. Thank God we were both with her when she passed but..."

Mrs. Avero hears her father-in-law tear up and now she wants to change the subject.

"I just thought of something. I have seen a plaque with 'The Italian Brotherhood' written on it, and I just remembered where I saw it. My God!" Anna says.

"Where did you see it?"

"Never mind. I will see if I can get this stopped. I'll call you later."

"Wait..."

Mrs. Avero doesn't want to discuss it further in case she is wrong about what she thinks she saw. She hangs up the phone and grabs her purse to look for a business card. After a few minutes of rifling through her purse, she finds it.

"Thank God!"

She picks up the phone, dials the number on the card, and makes an appointment for 4:00 that afternoon. She takes her purse, locks her office door, and walks to the reception area.

"Mrs. Petersen, I have an appointment at 4:00 today and I won't be back until tomorrow. Call me when Mrs. Fonte is here."

"She is already here with her mother in her mother's room."

"Good...Alright, we have some time. Let's give them some quiet time together before we call the psychologist."

Mrs. Petersen nods her head and sits down to go through some papers.

About a half hour later, Mrs. Avero goes to room 115. Chiara and Anna are watching television on the new television Chiara bought her for her room...of course with Anna's money. When they see Mrs. Avero, Anna smiles and Chiara stands up to kiss Mrs. Avero.

"Good morning, ladies. What are we watching?"

Chiara laughs. "The *Price is Right.*"

Anna is quiet as Mrs. Avero talks about her pregnancy. Chiara gives her some pregnancy advice.

"Well, Chiara. Let's leave your mother to finish her program and go into the hall for a few minutes so we don't disturb her."

Once in the hallway, out of Anna's listening range, Mrs. Avero says, "Chiara, let me take you to talk to our staff psychologist, Mrs. Ginsberg. She will bring you up to date on your mother's condition."

Chiara doesn't want to ask questions because she knows the answers will be upsetting. Mrs. Ginsberg's office door is open and she motions to Mrs. Avero and Chiara to come in and offers Mrs. Fonte a chair. Mrs. Avero looks at her watch and puts her hand on Chiara's shoulder.

"Mrs. Fonte, I have an appointment later. Before I leave, I'll check with you.

Chiara nods her head. She is beginning to feel overwhelmed. Mrs. Avero excuses herself, leaves the office, and closes the door. Mrs. Ginsberg takes the chair next to Chiara.

"Mrs. Fonte, your mother Anna is in a deep depression, as expected when someone enters a nursing home facility. We want to get her quickly acclimated. We suggest Anna not be taken out even for a Sunday country ride for a while because when she returns, the depression seems to worsen. Taking her out even for a few hours is a terrible reminder of what she will have to come back to."

Chiara isn't surprised her mother is in a depression. Who wouldn't be? She remembers when she and Joseph had to tell Anna of their plans to place her in a nursing home. Anna wasn't surprised. She knew her health was failing. She went to bed every night, praying she wouldn't wake up. Then there was the burden she was putting on Chiara's family, especially Dean, who had to take care of her much more now.

Anna could see how her children were sometimes at odds with each other, even when they tried to hide it. When she would meet with Joseph's mother Caterina, who was also a widow and lived with her daughter at the time, she confided to Caterina of her situation. It was easy to talk to Caterina because they could speak freely with each other in Italian. Anna confided that after all these years of taking care of her husband and family, she is now just a burden. Caterina, a couple of years later, could relate to Anna's situation because after living with her daughter Loretta and her family, Caterina had to move after her grandchildren were grown. Caterina now lives with a cousin in a small apartment behind their store almost an hour from her daughter. The lives of both Caterina Fonte and Anna Buonoforte are changing but for different reasons.

When Chiara and Joseph told Anna about the nursing home, their sons were not home. They didn't know how Anna would react when she heard the news.

"Ma, we have to take you to live somewhere where you will get constant care. We don't have what you need here. I will come almost every day. And if you can cooperate with the nursing home, on Sundays we will take you out to visit Giusepina, Rita, and wherever you would like to go."

Chiara had to stop talking because she saw the sorrow in Anna's face. Something she knew she would never forget. Anna just nodded and motioned to Chiara to lean over so she could kiss her. After that, Chiara had to leave the room.

Now, after Anna was in the nursing home, they could only take her out a few times, but Chiara kept her promise and tried to see her mother every day. Chiara doesn't care what the psychologist is suggesting. She knows how much her mother loves to go out and looks forward to it, but she can't contradict the psychologist.

"Mrs. Fonte, I suggest you and your siblings visit as much as you can. We are making your mother as comfortable as possible. Don't focus on the inevitable."

Chiara is fumbling with a tissue to calm herself as she speaks to Mrs. Ginsberg. "How can I not focus on what will happen? She is losing weight. When she is watching TV with the others, she has to be restrained. Now I understand she is incontinent and she must wear a damn diaper, but how humiliating! I would rather she die than live like that."

Mrs. Ginsberg sees Chiara is getting upset and will have to give her a dose of reality and priority. "Mrs. Fonte, I know this may sound harsh, but remember, you have a family, you have a husband and three children. What your mother is going through is her natural season that we all must go through. Mrs. Avero and I are doing everything we can to make your mother's quality of life the best it can be under the circumstances. You must continue doing what you're doing, but again, remember you have a life too. And your family needs you, probably more than your mother does at this point."

Mrs. Gisnberg walks to her desk, takes a pamphlet, and hands it to Chiara. "There is a new drug that is coming on the market from Hoffman-LaRoche. It's called Diazepam. It has very promising results in dealing with depression and it is subtle. If you agree, we can try it with your mother. It has had good results with our other patients who are using it."

Chiara scans through the pamphlet but can't focus on reading it. She just looks at the pictures of happy people, presumably after taking the drug. Mrs. Ginsberg looks at her watch and rises from her chair to signal the session is over.

"The other problem we are having is with your mother's eating. She won't wear her dentures and her food has to be cut up. It probably doesn't look that appetizing, especially to your mother, who I understand was an excellent cook. I know you and your mother are having lunch in the dining room, so let's head over there now."

At the door to the dining room, the two women stop. Mrs. Ginsberg gives a slight hug to Chiara. "Enjoy your lunch and stop in to see me anytime. I will let you know what effect the new drug is having on your mother. I am hoping it will be a great help to make her comfortable."

Sure, Chiara thought, *they'll just drug her up so she won't know what's going on. What a life.*

Chiara thanks her and walks into the dining room looking for her mother. Mrs. Petersen sees Chiara and goes over to greet her. She shakes Chiara's hand and walks her to her mother.

"How are you doing Mrs. Fonte?" Mrs. Petersen asks.

"After speaking to Mrs. Ginsberg, I am kinda upset."

"Well, doctors do that. Part of their job, I guess."

Chiara gave a slight smile.

"Mrs. Fonte, when we sit down with your mother, I suggest you don't say anything about eating. In our experience, sometimes it's a power thing. Like a child, it may be the only way they can rebel and show anger. Although I don't think in your mother's case that is what the problem is, I suggest some small talk about your husband and family. Ask her who has been here lately to visit and..."

Chiara interrupts. "I agree about the eating. It is probably what Mrs. Ginsberg said, but she has to eat. Why can't I bring her some home cooking?"

"One problem is that she either won't or can't eat without her dentures. What if you bring food in and she chokes? We are responsible. For that and other reasons, it's a rule that the residents eat what's made in the dining room. The New Jersey Health department has rules about food temperature and other things, but I have an idea. If you come here in the afternoon, there is no reason you can't bring her a meal and she can eat it in her room under your supervision. I think soups and soft macaroni would be a good idea."

Chiara agrees. "I have another question. My nephew is getting married. Is there any possibility that Momma could attend the wedding?"

Mrs. Petersen looks down for a second. "I know Mrs. Avero and Mrs. Ginsberg discussed taking her out. And well, there are two aspects to that question. First, it's the physical concern. You know she has hardening of the arteries and her equilibrium causes her to lose her balance. Also, she is incontinent and that could be an issue. The second aspect is mental. How will she handle leaving to go to a big celebration, seeing friends and family, and then returning here? Residents react differently to those experiences. Your mother is depressed for obvious reasons.

Perhaps you should talk to your sisters and brothers and you can all decide, rather than leaving it up to you alone. Maybe your nephew and his fiancé can visit before the wedding day."

Chiara nods her head in agreement but believes that probably won't happen. There won't be a visit. Chiara and Mrs. Petersen silently walk over to Anna and sit on either side of her. A waitress walks over to the table and introduces herself.

"Good afternoon. My name is Stella and I will be serving you today. I guess you are Anna's daughter?"

"Yes, I'm Chiara. What's for lunch today?"

"Today we have a choice of chicken and rice soup or a small salad with vinegarette dressing to start. Then we have meat loaf with mashed potatoes and peas or salmon with rice and peas. For dessert, we have Jello or rice pudding."

Chiara orders the chicken soup for herself and the soup and the meatloaf for her mother. Mrs. Petersen tells Chiara and Anna that she won't be eating and will leave them alone to have a nice meal. When she leaves, Chiara ignores Mrs. Ginsberg's advice and talks to her mother about eating.

"Ma, I am worried you are not eating."

"Who's hungry? Why should I eat? Wait till you see how the food comes."

"Why don't you wear your teeth? If they don't fit, I'll have Dr. Partenope make you a new set."

Anna just waves her hand. Then the chicken and rice soup came to the table. It had been put in a blender and it looked like white water. Anna pushes it away. Chiara puts a napkin around Anna's neck. Then Chiara tastes it and tries not to make a face.

"Ma, it's not that bad. How about we try it without the rice and a plain broth?"

Chiara calls over the waitress and asks to have just the broth.

"I'm sorry Mrs. Fonte. The soup comes with the rice and chicken already in it."

Chiara doesn't feel like arguing. When the waitress brings over the meat loaf, mashed potatoes, and peas, the meat loaf is mushed up with the gravy, and the peas are mushed up with the mashed potatoes. Chiara picks up the plate and takes it into the kitchen. "Excuse me. Can I have a regular serving of the meat loaf dinner?"

A big, brawny woman takes the plate from Chiara and looks at it. "This is how we are instructed to serve the food to residents who have no teeth so they don't choke."

Chiara is insistent. "I understand that, but please give me a regular order and I will cut it up for my mother."

The woman scowls at Chiara but Chiara will not back off.

"I will have to get permission from Mrs. Avero."

"Don't bother. Give me the meal and I will eat it."

"What about your mother?"

"I will worry about her. You just give me the meat loaf, mashed potatoes with the gravy on the side, and the peas."

"Ok. I'll bring it out."

"No need. I'll wait right here."

The woman shouts out the order and one of the assistant cooks gives the plate to Chiara. Chiara thanks him and brings the plate to her mother. She carefully cuts up the meat loaf, pours a little gravy over it, and lets her mother eat it. Anna eats the entire meal. Some of the staff watch as Anna eats. Then Chiara takes the empty plate, goes into the kitchen, and hands the plate to the supervisor.

"I don't care how you make the food for the others. I want my mother's food prepared the way I cut it up. Make believe that it's for your own mother."

"I hate my mother," says the supervisor. The staff laughs.

Chiara looks the woman up and down. "Then prepare it for whomever. I don't want my mother's meals massacred. I will inform my mother's goddaughter, Mrs. Avero, and..."

The woman's eyes widen. "That won't be necessary."

"That's great. For dessert, my mother would like Jello, whatever flavor you have, and some whipped cream on the side."

Chiara doesn't wait for a response. As she is leaving the kitchen, she sees the waitress, Stella, smiling. Chiara gives her a wink and sits next to her mother.

"Dessert is on its way!"

Anna leans over and kisses Chiara on the cheek and they both laugh. "You are just like your father."

Chiara enjoys hearing this but at the same time is sad. She realizes she is forgetting how her father's voice sounded and how he murdered the English language. Then she smiles to herself and holds her mother's hand as she eats the Jello. She will do whatever she has to, to make her mother as happy as she can be under the circumstances. She not only will do it for her mother, but more importantly, she will do it for her father. A few minutes later, they see Mrs. Petersen walking toward them.

"Well, it looks like you just finished your dessert. Was everything alright with the food?"

Before Anna can answer, Chiara speaks for her. "Oh yes. I just made a couple of small suggestions about my mother's diet and it is all settled."

"Wonderful. I have a meeting to go to, but I will check in and if there is anything you need, call me directly. Mrs. Avero told me to tell you to call her if you have any concerns or questions. She wanted to be here, but she had a very important appointment to go to."

Mrs. Petersen sees Anna looks a little happier than she has seen her before.

"I want to thank you and Mrs. Avero for all you've done," Chiara says.

Mrs. Petersen just nods and leaves, greeting some of the other residents.

Chapter 20
The Italian Brotherhood and Anna Avero, 1966

Mrs. Avero slowly gets out of her car and looks up at the large San Giorgio store sign over the front doors—San Giorgio and Family. She looks at her watch and remembers the last time she was here. This time, she is going to ask for a favor. As she walks toward the front doors, she wonders how she had ever had the nerve to confront them that first time. She has spoken to her father over the phone but hasn't been to the store since. She goes into the store and it's exactly like the first time she walked in, with the same smells, the same loud talking and arguing, cash registers ringing, and someone yelling for "a price check." Patrons are still running around, squeezing fruit, and cutting off each other with their shopping carts. She looks down an aisle and is surprised to see an old man has taken a can and is denting it with his foot. He goes around the corner to talk to a clerk who writes something on the can. She guesses it is discounted because of the dent. She walks toward the office and hears a large woman screaming at register four.

"I need a price check on Green Giant frozen corn, 12 ounces."

Then a response. "What size?"

"I said 12 ounces!"

Anna's half-brother Luca spots her and gives her a big hug. She is a little surprised. She wonders if they are still suspicious about her motives for visiting them and revealing who she is.

"Come on up to the office. We're wondering what you wanted to see us about," says Luca.

Uh, oh. Is there that suspicion again? she thinks. *It doesn't matter because they will find out soon enough why I am here, as well as a little surprise that involves all of them.*

She takes a deep breath and gently holds her stomach. When they get upstairs to the office, her father is waiting for her by the large picture window that overlooks the store. Instead of going directly over to him, she goes to the wall behind his desk where she remembers she had seen the plaque the last time she was in the office.

"Aha! I *did* see the Italian Brotherhood plaque on your wall!" Anna says.

Her father walks over to her and gives her a kiss and a hug. "What is this about?" he asks.

"Can I sit first? I'm a little tired."

Luca takes a chair for Mrs. Avero and she makes herself as comfortable as she can. "Well, it's kind of a long story," she says.

Mrs. Avero tells them all about Mrs. Fontanella and the possible lawsuit. Mr. San Giorgio, her father, sits on the edge of his desk looking down, twirling a pen in his hand. When Mrs. Avero finishes her story, he looks up at her.

"So, you want me to intervene and stop the lawsuit from going forward?"

At that moment, Morris comes up the stairs. "Hey. What's going on?" he asks.

"Your sister here is having a problem with someone at the Italian Brotherhood and wants to know if we can help," replies San Giorgio.

Mrs. Avero thinks for a moment that Morris probably thought she was here for money.

Mr. San Giorgio interrupts the silence. "Well, ordinarily I wouldn't hesitate, but there is a small problem."

Before he can say it, Morris blurts it out. "Art Dunatto."

Mr. San Giorgio gets up from the corner of his desk and sits behind it. "Yes. Art Dunatto. You see, that plaque was given to me to show their appreciation for our generosity and service. I was president for eight years. I left because there was a scandal with Art's son-in-law. He started working the bar and after a few months, the bar for the first time was losing money. It seemed we were ordering more and making less. It was a simple matter of bookkeeping. We had people start keeping a close watch on Art's son-in-law. We found out that when no one was looking, he would quickly pocket the money. Ya know, 'one for me, one for you' kinda thing. Someone ratted us out to Dunatto; that his son-in-law was being watched. We were about to go to the police and have him arrested. The problem was that Art got a few important people out of a jam and Art knew where the bodies, pardon the phrase, were buried. So, they settled for just not allowing Art's son-in-law to work or enter the club if we dropped it, and Art agreed. He really had no choice. However, I disagreed and then pressure was put on me and some others. For the club's sake to avoid possible bad publicity, I resigned and was given a big dinner and that plaque. I never spoke to Art or some of the others again and haven't stepped into the club since."

Mrs. Avero looks down and nods her head.

"That, my dear daughter, does not mean I will not help you. On the contrary. It will be with great pleasure I help you and get back at that son-of-a bitch, but not in the way you think."

Mrs. Avero looks around as Luca and Morris laugh. She is confused.

Mr. San Giorgio walks around the desk to Mrs. Avero, sits on the edge, and puts his hand on top of hers. "Honey, it doesn't matter what happened to me. I was getting sick of the club because it was getting too political. I know of Mrs. Fontanella. She has quite a reputation, and she will not go away quietly, even with a phone call. She will make her husband's life miserable *and* then they will try to make *your* life miserable. If she wants to go to court, then that is what you should do...as harsh as it sounds. She needs to be taught a lesson. In this kind of case, you're going to have a jury. Her lawyer, Art Dunatto, is a dope and I am sure Mrs. Fontanella is going to make a fool of herself with outbursts, or whatever, and juries don't like that. Like I said, this woman needs some-one to challenge her 'holier than thou' attitude. People get intimidated and nervous because of the cost of lawyers, so they back down and the Fontanellas get their way. They really must be confronted once and for all."

"Yes, but it is at *our* expense," Mrs. Avero says.

"Do you trust me?"

"What do you mean?"

"I'll tell you what...who is taking the case? Your husband's law firm?"

"Yes. He's a partner at his father's law firm...but he earned the partnership and..."

"Oh, I am sure. Have your husband's father call me and we'll talk it over. I promise you it will turn out in your favor and be completely legal but with a small twist. We will try to have an honest judge preside over the case and not one of Art's flunky drinking buddies. Dunatto won't expect that. Also, let us know when the case comes to court and me and the boys here will be in the first row. That will rattle him. They are not the only ones who can intimidate people."

"Well, there's something else," Mrs. Avero says. She looks around to see if she can tell if there is any sign of suspicion on their faces. "Well...Luca and Morris...you are going to be uncles and you, dear father, are going to be a grandfather."

Hearing this news, they all yell at once, which startles her. Then the yelling turns to laughing. She stands up so they can hug her.

"This calls for a proper celebration. I want you to come to our house with your husband to meet my mother and the rest of the family. It's time. Promise me. This other matter will take care of itself, don't worry. I promise," Mr. San Giorgio says.

She nods, but there is something she hasn't told them and it may ruin everything. Something she will have to take care of first, which may be a problem. Now that she sees they are good people, her fear is that when they find out what she is hiding, and that she hasn't been completely truthful, she may lose them all once again. But for now, all is well.

Before Luca and Morris can walk Mrs. Avero out of the store, she stops for a bathroom break and when she comes out, Morris and Luca take her arms as they walk into the parking lot.

"You don't know how happy you made us, especially our father, with your news. By the way, Grandmother is in Florida so I don't know if she'll be back in time, but don't worry, she will want to meet you when she returns," says Luca.

Mrs. Avero stops for a second and turns to face Luca. "Listen, there is something I didn't tell our father or any of you. I already met with your grandmother...well our grandmother. That may sound a little sneaky, but I had to be sure of the situation and what type of reception I would get. I also have been in touch with her in Florida. If your grandmother didn't want anything to do with me or my mother, then I wouldn't have taken it any further. You see, I couldn't take a chance because there is something I haven't told your father. I was so mad when we first met. I lied and told him my mother had died, but she is quite alive. Please keep it quiet. I don't want him to know until I bring her."

Luca and Morris give her a hug, being careful of her stomach, and they all laugh. Luca takes her two hands in his. "I am so happy that we found you...or you found us. Between us, we have not seen our father so happy in such a long time. I know this is terrible to say, he loved our mother, but I really believe your mother was, is, the love of his life. The only sadness is he thinks she is dead, but you have no idea how happy he will be when he finds out she is alive," says Luca.

Mrs. Avero is surprised to hear how her father feels about her mother after all this time. "He talks about her?" she asks.

Luca looks down for a few seconds. "After you left, he told us the whole story in more detail and how, for years, he was so ashamed. It was a big burden taken off his shoulders to see you and how great you turned out. He is going to go nuts when he sees her."

Mrs. Avero looks up, shaking her head. "I just hope my mother feels the same way."

They nervously laugh and Luca helps Mrs. Avero into her car and watches her as she drives out of the parking lot.

The boys look at each other and laugh. Morris slaps Luca on his back. "Life is friggin weird man!"

"You can say that again!"

"Life is friggin weird man!"

"Oh, shut up!"

Arms around each other's shoulders, they walk back into the store.

Chapter 21
A Reunion of Sorts

Mrs. Avero hears her mother yawn as she answers the phone. "Good morning, Mom! I hope I didn't wake you up."

"No. I heard you leave the house, and I made breakfast for your husband. Good eater!"

"I know he is, and he doesn't gain a pound. I look at a piece of pizza and it goes right to my hips."

"Well... you are six months pregnant. That should count, you know."

"Yeah. I am looking like a baby hippo."

"Don't be ridiculous."

"Well, I didn't call to talk about my weight. Speaking of food, I want to take you to lunch, but we have to make a stop first. I want you to meet someone."

"Who?"

"It's a surprise." Mrs. Avero rolls her eyes to heaven and prays that what she has planned is not a bad idea.

"We are going someplace nice for lunch, so put on a nice dress and full make-up."

Mrs. Avero wants her mother to look her best for the "reunion." She hopes her mother is not suspicious. How can she be? This reunion will be the farthest thing from her mind. Even so, she wants her to look her best, but her mother is still objecting.

"You're kidding? In the middle of the day?"

"Never mind. Just do it. I will pick you up at 10:30."

Before her mother can object again, she hangs up the phone. Then she thinks, *I hope this isn't a mistake. Even if it is, at least things will be resolved one way or the other.*

Mrs. Avero walks out of her office to tell Mrs. Petersen that she will be leaving at about 10:00 and will be back after lunch. Mrs. Petersen is waving a piece of paper.

"Your father-in-law has been trying to reach you. He called the house and said the phone was busy. You are to call him at this number as soon as you get in."

"I hope a time doesn't come when you can get calls in your car or wherever you are. How terrible that would be!"

Mrs. Avero takes the paper back to her office and dials the number.

"Good morning, Judge Myer's Office. How can I help you?

"Hello. This is Mrs. Avero..."

Before she can finish, the secretary hands the phone to her father-in-law.

"Anna. Finally. I'm here with a friend of mine, Judge Lucy Meyer, and we're discussing how to handle this lawsuit. We were just served the papers yesterday."

Anna is getting frustrated, partly because of her raging pregnant hormones.

"Why didn't you call me?"

Her father-in-law can hear the frustration in her voice. "Why bother you until I knew more? Unfortunately, I know more now and this is going to be a pain in the ass. Judge Meyer doesn't think the Fontanellas have a case since it is her word against yours."

Anna calmed down. "All I tried to do was save her mother. No good deed goes unpunished. Jesus," says Anna. "I'm telling you, if it is up to me, I am not giving in. That woman is not getting her way."

"Well, I don't think that matters anymore because we understand that Mrs. Fontanella's mother moved in with her cousin. I really don't know how happy she is, but at least she isn't being put in the nursing home."

"Thank God! Then what does Fontanella want?" asks Anna.

"Maybe an apology, but Judge Meyer thinks at this point she may want a money settlement."

"Well, that's not going to happen."

"Anna, we have to look at this rationally and practically. Just in legal fees, even if it's our own people, it will not be worth it."

"I don't care. It's the principle of the matter. Anyway, there may be another solution. Did Mr. San Giorgio call you about the case?"

"Oh yeah, I got a message that he called. What is that about? Who is he?"

"I told you he is my birth father."

"By the way, did you ever tell your mother you met up with him?"

Anna rolls her eyes, knowing how she is going to tell her mother. "She is going to find out very soon. But besides that, don't do anything until you talk to my father. He is connected to the Italian Brotherhood and has some ideas; all legal." *At least I hope they will be legal,* she thinks to herself.

"What kind of ideas?"

"I don't know. Just talk to him before you make any kind of decision about settling. You know, settling can set a bad precedent. It might be looked at as an admission of guilt."

"Wow. My daughter-in-law, the lawyer! Anyway, I just found out this case is on the docket for next year."

"Let's just get this behind us," Anna says in a more peaceful tone. "Dad, I'll call you tonight."

"OK. Stay well, dear. It's my grandchild you're carrying around."

"Oh, thanks! I guess I don't count!"

"You know what I mean!"

Mrs. Avero laughs and hangs up the phone. She looks at her watch and decides to pick her mother up earlier to make sure she is dressed properly. When Mrs. Avero arrives at her house, her mother is already dressed, and sitting on the porch. She gets out of the car, wondering again if she is doing the right thing.

"Wow! You're all dressed and you look so nice!"

"You know how I hate to be late."

"You look very pretty...and young! Perfect!"

Mrs. Avero's mother ignores the compliment. "Now, who are we meeting?"

"An old friend. Don't worry."

It is Mrs. Avero who is worrying. Mr. San Giorgio thinks her mother is *dead*. Is he going to be mad that she lied to him or elated that they are reunited? How will her mother react? Under her breath, Mrs. Avero voices her concern.

"I hope I am doing the right thing, but I don't have a choice."

Her mother hears her whisper. "What did you say, dear?"

"Oh. I think I should pee before we leave."

"That's a good idea. When I was pregnant with you, I was always on the toilet."

When Mrs. Avero comes back, she helps her mother in the car. Before she puts her purse in the backseat, she sneakily takes out a piece of paper with an address she has memorized to double check she remembers correctly. When she gets in the driver's seat, her mother asks her again.

"Can't you tell me where we are going?"

"Don't worry, Mom. Just going to visit an old friend."

"And where does this old friend live?"

"In Alpine. It's a small town near the Hudson."

Mrs. Avero's mother doesn't ask any more questions. Mrs. Avero goes over the instructions in her head that were all worked out. She had made a call and confirmed the time before they left.

When they pull up to the address Mrs. Avero was given, she has to look at the paper in her pocket to make sure she is at the right house.

"My God, Anna! Who lives here?"

Mrs. Avero doesn't respond; she is in shock. There is a long driveway up to the house that ends in a circular driveway. The house is in the Tudor style, with turrets and gables and a large fountain in the middle that looks like something out of the seventeenth century, with Italian sculptures spouting water. Mrs. Avero slowly pulls around the front of the house outside the front door and parks.

"Anna, where are we?"

"Don't worry, Mom."

As Mrs. Avero parks the car, the front door opens and there stands Morris San Giorgio. Morris greets Mrs. Avero with a kiss and opens the door for Mrs. Avero's mother to get out of the car. Morris takes her hand and introduces himself.

"Good morning. I'm Morris."

Mrs. Avero's mother returns the greeting. She is puzzled and looks at Mrs. Avero. As they walk up the stairs to the entrance of the house, Morris whispers in Mrs. Avero's ear, "Pop is on the phone in the kitchen. We're keeping him busy. It was a real chore to keep him here."

She looks at Morris and whispers back, "I hope it's worth it. Maybe I should have kept the car running."

They look at each other and smile as they enter a huge foyer with double staircases. At the top of the stairs, a large stained-glass window floods the foyer with colored lights as the sun shines through it.

Morris leads them into the living room to the right of the staircase. "Please, this way, and have a seat. I will be right back," he says.

Mrs. Avero's mother is silent. She helps her mother to a couch and they sit down.

"Anna, what is this about?"

"Mom, I have something to tell you. Maybe I should have told you first, but I was afraid. Whatever happens, please be calm, and I will explain."

As Mrs. Avero asks her mother to stay calm, Morris walks in with his father. Mr. San Giorgio first goes to Mrs. Avero and gives her a hug and a kiss. "How's my grandchild in there?"

He moves to greet Mrs. Avero's mother. "And who do we..."

He stops mid-sentence. He looks at Mrs. Avero, then again at her mother, and tries to say something. "What, who..."

Mrs. Avero's mother stands up and slowly walks to Mr. San Giorgio and looks into his blue eyes. He backs up a bit. Neither speaks for a few seconds. The silence is broken when Mrs. Avero's mother slaps Mr. San

Giorgio across the face. Everyone freezes in place, and then Mrs. Avero's mother slaps him again. Mr. San Giorgio stands there.

After a second, he yells, "What was that for? Anna, what is this about?"

"I'm sorry. I lied. My mother is obviously alive, and she just slapped you."

"I know that, but what for?"

Her eyes burning, Anna's mother stands in front of Mr. San Giorgio. "Why didn't you ever try to contact me? Were you so afraid of your parents that you couldn't be a man and at least part ways amicably?"

Anna speaks up to make the situation better, but instead, it goes the wrong way. "Ma, it wasn't his parent's fault. He ran away because he was too young and too scared."

A second later, Anna realizes from her mother's reaction that telling her the truth was a mistake. Anna's mother slaps Mr. San Giorgio again.

"Coward! All that time went by. All I knew was heartbreak, and you ran away." She turns to Anna. "Anna, what were you thinking?!"

Anna's mother storms out of the house and sits in the car. Anna apologizes and says she has to leave and will call or something. When Anna gets in the car, her mother again asks her the same question; this time through her tears.

"Anna, what were you thinking? I would run up to him like nothing ever happened?"

Anna is silent. She starts the car and pulls out of the driveway. Morris comes out of the house, hoping they will come back in. He just waves to them, not even knowing why.

"Anna! I am asking you! What were you thinking?!"

Anna pulls into a Seven-Eleven store and parks. She looks at her mother and explains how she got the information that Enzo Buonoforte was holding from Chiara Fonte.

"Mother, you ask what was I thinking? What were you all thinking? Why were you all lying to me all my life?"

Her mother calms down hearing what Anna is saying about the situation. She wants to explain.

"Those were the times. A scandal like that could ruin a family's reputation. Your grandparents thought it was the best thing to do then. It was just the times."

Anna knows that would be her explanation, but she wants to hear it from her mother, who stares out the car window. Then her mother surprises her.

"Take me back to their house."

"Now! Don't you think that's a little premature considering you just beat up Mr. San Giorgio?"

"Mr. San Giorgio needed to be hit for what he did. He's lucky I didn't punch him in his big nose!"

Anna's mother keeps looking out the car window. It is easier to tell Anna the truth without facing her.

"Seeing him after all these years, I still love him. I guess I will always love him. The bastard!"

She turns to Anna. "I know you were trying to do the right thing." She shakes her right hand. "My hand hurts! Boy! I really slugged him!"

They laugh and Anna's mother moves over and embraces her daughter. Anna starts the car and heads back to the San Giorgio house. When she arrives at the house, she blows the horn. She tries to at least give them some warning.

"Ma, wait here. Let me see what the mood is inside."

Anna is about to ring the doorbell when Morris opens the door. "Oh. Thank God you're back."

Anna shakes her head. "She loves him."

Chapter 22
Bergen County Court House. Hackensack, New Jersey, Summer, 1967

"Counselor...Mr. Dunatto, please tell your client that if there is *one more outburst,* your client is not only going to pay a hefty fine and be incarcerated, but I may just dismiss this case and hold you in contempt as well. Do you understand, counselor?"

"Uhhh, me Your Honor?"

The judge looks at Mrs. Fontanella's lawyer, smiles, and slowly nods her head.

"Mr. Russo, you can continue with your opening remarks."

"Thank you, Your Honor. The elderly; how do we take care of our elderly? One way is to just put them away in a nursing home."

Mr. Dunatto quickly stands up. "I object, Your Honor, with the term, 'put them away.'"

"Objection sustained. And you don't have to stand up every time you object. Please continue Mr. Russo."

Before he sits down, Mr. Dunatto looks back at the gallery and again sees that Mr. San Giorgio and his two sons are sitting behind Mrs. Avero's lawyers. As Mr. San Giorgio predicted, Mr. Dunatto is getting rattled.

He whispers to Mrs. Fontanella, "What the hell are the San Giorgio's doing here?"

Mrs. Fontanella looks over and shrugs her shoulders. She doesn't even know who they are.

Mr. Russo continues, "Again, thank you, Your Honor. Some of us responsibly take care of our elderly parents, or in many cases a surviving parent, by taking them in or taking care of them the way they took care of us. It is only to the point when circumstances do not allow the elderly to take care of themselves, or if the elderly have health issues and they need constant care, that the elderly should be *placed...*"

Mr. Russo looks directly at Mr. Dunatto and the judge smiles and nods. As Mr. San Giorgio promised through his connections, he was able to have an honest judge take the case who wouldn't stand for any nonsense.

Mr. Russo continues, "...who only then should be placed in a proper facility that can take care of the elderly around the clock. In this case, we have a woman, Mrs. Fontanella's mother, Mrs. Concetta Voulo, who is fully capable of taking care of herself and does not need any nursing home assistance. We will illustrate through witnesses and Mrs. Voulo's own testimony..."

Mr. Dunatto turns to Mrs. Fontanella. "What does he mean testify *herself?* Where is your mother?"

"I spoke to her yesterday. She is down the Jersey shore. They'll never find her."

Mr. Russo looks directly at Mrs. Fontanella and goes on, "... despite this fine, capable woman who is fully able to take care of herself... her daughter, Mrs. Lori Fontanella, was willing to *put her away* and why..."

"Again, Your Honor, I object to the term, 'put her away.'"

"Mr. Russo, we understand where you are going, but for the sake of expediency, get to the point and please don't use the term, 'put her away.' Objection sustained."

"Yes, Your Honor. My apologies. Again, we will show through witnesses and her own..."

Mr. Russo is interrupted by the courtroom door opening. A dozen or so people came into the courtroom talking and trying to figure out where to sit. The judge brings down her gavel and calls out to the bailiff.

"Quiet in this courtroom. Bailiff, have these people find a seat, so we are not here until Christmas. Thank you."

Some people start to apologize for the noise as they are sitting.

Mrs. Fontanella stands up and turns to the people who just entered the courtroom. "Mother, what are you doing here? How can you..."

"Mr. Dunatto. Please control your client. It seems she is surprised a witness has shown up. What is going on and who are all these people?"

Mrs. Avero's father-in-law speaks up. "Your Honor. I know some of these people. May I..."

"It isn't necessary, but I find Mrs. Fontanella's reaction to some of them interesting. Not another word, Mrs. Fontanella, unless I alone ask you something."

Mrs. Fontanella's lawyer has his hand on her shoulder, ready to push her down if she gets up again.

"Now, without getting hysterical, Mrs. Fontanella, who do you recognize?" the judge asks.

"Excuse me, Your Honor, but I see my mother and her cousins are here. I don't know the other people."

"Well thank you, Mrs. Fontanella. See how easy this is? What is your mother's name?"

"Concetta Voulo, Your Honor."

"Mr. Russo, do you know who these other people are?" the judge asks.

"Your Honor, the women next to Mrs. Fontanella's mother are her two cousins and the man next to them is Mrs. Fontanella's mother's psychologist. The young man in the wheelchair is Danny, who is in residence at the Paramus Nursing Home and may be called as a future character witness for Mrs. Avero."

The judge goes through her papers to find Danny's name to see if he is mentioned in the legal case brief, but he is not listed. Mr. Russo gestures to the people in the gallery to sit down.

"The rest are some of the staff of the nursing home and are here as character witnesses to support and testify to Mrs. Avero's outstanding dedication, work ethic, and passion for what she does at the Paramus Nursing Home. The young woman with the gray sweater is Mrs. Petersen, who is here as a witness for Mrs. Avero. She was working at a desk right outside Mrs. Avero's office the day Mrs. Fontanella had a discussion with Mrs. Avero about Mrs. Fontanella wanting to have her mother *placed* in the nursing home. Since it was a contentious discussion, we want to have Mrs. Petersen available to collaborate Mrs. Avero's testimony, if necessary," Mr. Russo says.

Mrs. Fontanella's lawyer quickly stands up. "Your Honor..."

"Counselor, were you aware of all this in the discovery phase of the trial? You seem surprised by Mrs. Fontanella's mother's attendance."

"Your Honor, I am surprised to see Mrs. Petersen. She was not on the witness list."

"Mr. Russo, is that true?"

"Your Honor, Mrs. Petersen was out of town attending to her ill mother, and it is only at the last minute that it is possible for her to attend the trial."

"What about a deposition? Was she deposed?" asks the judge.

"Again, Your Honor, she had to leave suddenly before we had time to depose her. We were not able to fly to Florida before the trial for her deposition, but she was able to leave her mother and fly up for the trial."

Mr. Dunatto looks around the room and then whispers to Mrs. Fontanella before addressing the judge. "Your Honor, under the circumstances, may I have time to confer with my client on a few issues that just came to light before we continue?"

"I think you better. I'm glad you're not pleading a case for me." The judge looks at her watch.

"Alright, it is 11:35. A little early for lunch, but I see the jury appears a little antsy and may need a break. We'll take a break until 1:00 sharp. And I mean sharp. We have more important cases to hear. Court is adjourned. The jury is excused. Bailiff, clear the court."

"Everyone rise," says the Bailiff.

As soon as the judge leaves the bench, a wave of talking begins. The jury looks over at Mrs. Fontanella, who has been instructed not to make eye contact. Mrs. Fontanella wants to get up to find out why her mother is there, but instead, Mr. Dunatto quickly leads her out of the room and into an adjoining conference room. Mrs. Fontanella sits. Mr. Dunatto closes the door, takes a chair, and sits right in front of her.

"Did you know that the woman, Mrs. Petersen, was sitting outside the room when you were talking to Mrs. Avero?"

"What does that matter?"

"Are you kidding? It matters a great deal. This woman, this Mrs. Petersen, is a witness who can collaborate with everything Mrs. Avero says. This woman can attest to anything Mrs. Avero will say as the truth and deny anything that you say. She can even lie."

"She wouldn't!"

"Oh, no? You are asking for a million dollars in damages, which you won't even get a tenth of. You don't think someone would lie to save their ass? Are you kidding? Now think. Was she sitting outside the room when you and Mrs. Avero were talking?"

"Well, not when I went in. She escorted me to Mrs. Avero and brought in a file. Then there was some commotion, and she was there when I left. I don't remember if she was there the whole time. Why would I even care if she was there at the time?"

"Did you not hear me when I said she could collaborate what Mrs. Avero said and even lie?"

"I don't like your tone, Mr. Dunatto, and..."

"Right now, I don't give a shit whether you like my tone or not. This whole case has turned around and lady you better care what Mrs. Petersen says because now it's two people's words against yours, *and* your mother *and* her head shrinker are here and he is going to testify that your mother is no candidate for a nursing home."

Mrs. Fontanella quickly realizes that things are out of control and her lawyer is not pulling his punches. Mr. Dunatto pulls his chair closer to her and speaks in a whisper.

"I know you had another psych evaluate your mother, who said she *was* qualified to be in a nursing home, but the judge can get a court-appointed expert. Only that won't be necessary because your mother's cousin is going to testify that your mother is more than happy to live with her and is thriving, cooking, going out to do whatever old ladies do! AND that poor kid in the wheelchair, Danny? He looks like something out of a Rockwell painting. And he is MY client, so there may even be a conflict of interest."

Mrs. Fontanella is about to say something but just looks up and shakes her head.

"Don't look up to heaven for help. I think we're fucked. Your damn husband told me this is a 'slam dunk' and your mother would never testify even though she was on the list because they were going to settle!"

"I told her not to show up."

"She has to testify because she was given a subpoena! They're all here!"

"But I told her not to testify, and she agreed. We sent her to Atlantic City for the summer. No one knew where she was."

"Well, they found her, and she has to testify and tell the truth. Now guess who is having the last laugh!"

Mr. Dunatto gets out of his chair and paces the floor, trying to decide what to do. "Ok, ok. We have two choices. First, you drop the case and you pay for Mrs. Avero's lawyer's fees and possible court costs. I just want to get out of this as fast as I can."

"WHAT! I am not going to do that. I want another lawyer. You're fired!"

"Fine, that's the second choice. You can continue with this bullshit lawsuit and you don't have to fire me because I quit! And if, and I mean if, you can even find another lawyer, those people in the back of the court with pen and paper in hand are reporters and they are chomping at the bit to report on this. No lawyer will touch this. Somebody called the reporters in and it wasn't me. So, you will not only lose the case, but you will lose your reputation. Or are you too stupid to get it?!"

"How dare you...!"

Mr. Dunatto grabs a chair again and sits right in Mrs. Fontanella's face. "Listen, lady. Let me make this very, very clear. If you don't drop this case, not only will *your* reputation be shot, but so will your husband's. His insurance clients will go 'bye-bye.' When it gets out that his wife wanted to throw her mother out and stick her in a nursing home that she is not suited to be in, AND she wants to have a poor guy in a wheelchair, who looks like a poster kid for Muscular Dystrophy, thrown into the streets, AND that I am his trustee, which is again going to be seen as a conflict of interest..."

Mrs. Fontanella stands up. "I never wanted him thrown out into the street. My point is that if there is room enough for a young person then there is room for my mother!"

"And it is a stupid point! God. You still don't get it, do you? The reporters will twist it any way they want. Just the fact that he is *here* is bad enough, and that is the defendant's point. You and your husband will be torn apart in the papers!"

Mrs. Fontanella sits back down. "But you said he wasn't on the witness list."

"He isn't a witness. He is here to make you look like a monster, and that is what you look like with these witnesses and the other people out there. Don't you get it? Russo and the other lawyers intentionally brought them in just to intimidate us, and it is a great visual for the jury and the press. With this circus going on, you're gonna be a media star. Maybe if you're lucky, you'll make it on the five o'clock local TV news. Who knows! Maybe Cronkite will pick it up! And why again didn't your husband show up? Huh?"

Mrs. Fontanella's face goes white and her body goes limp. "I, I just thought..."

"Yeah. Stupid me. I just thought too. Well, I'm thinking again and I am getting out of this. Either you drop this and go out with some dignity, or I go out there and hold a little news conference about why I quit. You have five seconds to make up your mind."

Mrs. Fontanella goes into her purse for a hankie and cries.

"That's good. Let the judge see you came to your senses and reconsidered. Now sit here. I will let the court know we are reconsidering and may want to drop the case. I need a few minutes to write a statement or something, so we don't look like two fools."

Mr. Dunatto leaves the room. Mrs. Fontanella can see out the door that her husband finally has shown up and is talking to the bailiff while walking toward the conference room. As he comes into the conference room, he sees his wife is upset.

"Lorileigh, what happened?"

"It is all over. It's a mess. We have to drop the case. Didn't you see my mother, her cousin, and my mother's psychiatrist sitting out there? They are all going to testify against me."

"You said she wouldn't testify. We sent her away for the summer. How the hell did they find her?"

"Well, they found her and the other damn lawyer gave my mother and her cousin a subpoena to show up, and they are here. You said they would settle. Well, guess what? My mother *is* going to testify. It's all over with. We even have to pay legal fees."

"What! I am not going to pay legal fees! We are going to fight this! We'll get another lawyer."

Mr. Dunatto comes into the room and breaks in as Mr. Fontanella is yelling. "You're going to have to get another lawyer, if you can find one because your lawyer... me...is going to quit if we don't drop the case, your lawyer...me...is going to meet with the reporters."

Mrs. Fontanella's husband slams his hand on the table, startling both Mrs. Fontanella and Mr. Dunatto.

"I don't care. We'll get another lawyer. I have connections. We're going to fight this."

There is a knock on the door, and the bailiff walks in. "Excuse me. Court is about to reconvene."

Mr. Dunatto walks over to the bailiff. "Things may have changed. I would like to have a word with the judge. I'll be out in a few minutes."

The bailiff nods his head and closes the door.

Mr. Fontanella walks over to Mr. Dunatto. "Wait one minute, Dunatto. You said they would settle. We are not dropping the case. Do you hear?"

Mr. Dunatto grabs Mr. Fontanella's arm, slightly opens the door, and makes him peer out into the courtroom.

"Look. Take a good look."

Mr. Dunatto squeezes Mr. Fontanella's arm hard and makes sure he sees his pointing finger.

"There is your mother-in-law looking like she stepped out of Life Magazine about a story of how a perfectly able old woman and the elderly are tossed aside and forced to live in nursing homes. Can you imagine that? And look at the back of the courtroom. Can you see those people with the pen and paper? You think they are taking drink orders? No. They are there to ruin the both of you and your business. Because if you don't drop this case, that is what I will help them do because I am not going down with you on this...on this 'slam dunk' easy money court case, as you so smugly put it. And don't be surprised if the nursing home doesn't counter-sue for defamation!"

Mr. Fontanella whispers to himself, " *We thought they would settle.*"

"Not after I heard *Clarence Darrow's* opening statement and saw those witnesses showing up," says Mr. Dunatto.

Mrs. Fontanella's husband turns to her as she is looking for another hankie in her purse. "Lorileigh, I thought you said your mother would never show up."

Mrs. Fontanella is talking through her tears. "I don't know...I don't know what happened...I just don't...Maybe we should have stopped this when they said they wouldn't settle. Oh, God."

Mr. Dunatto is out of patience. "Well, kids. What is it? Do I talk to the judge or the reporters?"

Mr. Fontanella is right in Mr. Dunatto's face. "You will never talk to the reporters. I will ruin you. You'll see. You'll never get another client."

Mr. Dunatto walks away. "Are you kidding? After this case, I probably won't anyway. And by the way, you told me you could fix which judge would take this case. Look who we got: A 'bitch on wheels' who probably wants to send us to jail! You have five seconds to decide."

Mrs. Fontanella's husband yells and hits the conference table so hard with his hand that it startles a couple of people in the courtroom, sending the bailiff in to see what is happening.

"Is everything alright in here?" the bailiff asks. He looks around the room and they just stare at him. "By the way, the judge is coming back in a few minutes to reconvene." The bailiff leaves and gently shuts the door.

Mr. Dunatto leans against the door. "So...what is it?"

Mr. Fontanella looks out the window wishing he never got involved. "Drop it."

"Ok..."

The bailiff comes into the conference room and tells them the judge is coming back into the courtroom.

"All rise," the bailiff says.

The judge walks in and everyone sits down.

"I understand, Mr. Dunatto, that there has been a new development in the case. Would you like to share that with the court?"

"Yes, Your Honor. After considerable thought, and consideration for the court's time, my client has decided to..."

Mr. Fontanella, who is sitting with his wife, suddenly stands up. "We are not dropping the case..."

There is a collective gasp and talking in the courtroom. The judge brings down her gavel several times and calls for order.

"I said quiet, everyone! Mr. Dunatto, who is this man disturbing my courtroom with his loud outburst?"

"I am sorry, Your Honor. This is *Mr. Martino Fontanella*, Mrs. Fontanella's husband."

Mr. Dunatto puts his hand on Mr. Fontanella's shoulder, forces him to sit down, and leans over him.

The judge addressed Mr. Fontanella, "Sir, stay seated and keep your mouth shut. This is a courtroom and not a sporting event. Now, Mr. Dunatto, what is it? Are you dropping the case or not?"

"Can you give me just a moment, Your Honor?

"You have sixty seconds and if I hear any more talking, I am going to clear the courtroom and declare a mistrial."

Mr. Dunatto huddles with his clients and after a few seconds, he stands tall and addresses the judge. "Your Honor, the Fontanellas want to continue with the court case."

There is a sudden burst of talking by everyone in the courtroom. The judge again brings down her gavel.

"I said quiet. Bailiff, get ready to get security to empty the courtroom. Continue Mr. Dunatto."

"Your Honor, after conferring with my clients and with their desire to continue with the case, I am respectfully going to resign. I don't feel under the circumstances that I can properly serve my clients in light of new developments. Again, I don't feel I can properly serve my clients."

You can hear a pin drop in the courtroom.

"I would like to see both lawyers in my chambers...now!" says the judge.

The judge gets up from her seat and the bailiff calls for everyone to rise. As the lawyers walk into the judge's chambers, Mr. Dunatto goes in last and wipes the sweat from his face with his hankie.

Lawyers for both sides stand in front of the judge.

"People, what is going on here?"

Mr. Dunatto speaks first. "Your Honor, under the circumstances..."

"Mr. Dunatto, we got that already with your little speech. Be more specific. My patience is running low."

Mr. Dunatto continues, "Your Honor, one aspect is the boy, Danny. I am his trustee and I feel it may be a conflict of interest in this case."

"He isn't a witness, and he isn't even in the brief," says the judge.

"Well, Your Honor, it was when Mrs. Fontanella saw him in the nursing home that she felt if they had room for him, then *what about my mother*?"

Mr. Russo broke in. "Your Honor, may I interrupt for a moment?"

"Please."

"Well, we brought Danny in as a future witness to testify on Mrs. Avero's care for him and..."

Now the judge interrupts. "Come on. You have him here for a visual and to intimidate Mr. Dunatto's client, which at this point didn't work because they do not want to drop the case. Then again, there's the jury who are eating this up. Mr. Dunatto, it seems you were surprised by Mrs. Fontanella's mother and the others showing up because..."

Mr. Dunatto interrupts the judge. "Your Honor, I advised my client to drop the case. Again, I cannot properly serve them. Under the circumstances, I do not believe they have a chance to win."

"Alright then. Enough with 'under the circumstances.' You're out and we will reschedule so the Fontanella's can hire another lawyer. Thank you everyone. Let's go back in."

"Everyone please rise," the bailiff says.

"I would like to thank the jury for their attendance, even though we are not moving forward with the case at this time. Let me look at my schedule to see when we can reschedule and..."

"Your Honor."

"Yes, Mr. Dunatto."

"My clients want to put in a request for a change of venue because..."

"Motion denied...Now let's see. We will reconvene two weeks from today on the 15th at 9:00 am. The jury is excused and court is adjourned."

Mr. Dunatto is putting his papers in his briefcase when he is interrupted by Mr. Fontanella.

"So, you're quitting."

"I told the judge I cannot properly serve you because you're two stupid and stubborn assholes and I don't want to be involved in such a sorry ass losing case. And don't worry. I won't speak to any reporters because I don't want to be associated with anything that has to do with you two and this fucking case. Good luck."

Mr. Dunatto stands up, closes his briefcase, and is ready to leave. In parting he says to the Fontanellas, "*And* you will receive my bill and if you don't pay it, then I will see you in court again, and I will speak to the reporters *then*. And again, good luck!"

Mr. Dunatto walks over to Mr. Russo, Mrs. Avero, and Mrs. Avero's father-in-law. "Good job, guys!"

Mr. Russo, Mrs. Avero, and her father-in-law give a slight, embarrassed grin. Mrs. Avero breaks the silence. "You were smart, wanting to drop the case, Art. Are you *really* quitting?"

"Like a hot potato. By the way, if your firm needs another lawyer, give me a call. I would love to work with you guys."

Mr. Dunatto looks over at the Fontanellas who are getting ready to leave and walks past them without saying a word. At this point, no one else is leaving the courtroom, including Mrs. Fontanella's mother and cousin.

Anna whispers to her husband, "We gave up taking the baby out for this!"

They shake their heads.

"Well, at least your mother watching the baby is having a good time," her husband replies.

Mrs. Fontanella stands up, looks at her husband, and then at the judge who is still sitting at her bench going through some papers and talking to the bailiff.

"Your Honor?"

The judge looks at Mrs. Fontanella with reluctance to answer her.

"Yes...Mrs. Fontanella."

"We're dropping the case."

The courtroom suddenly breaks out with gasps and whispers. The judge brings down the gavel.

"Quiet in my courtroom. Quiet or I'll clear the room and none of you will hear what Mrs. Fontanella has to say, which I am sure we're all dying to hear. Continue Mrs. Fontanella."

There is dead silence. Even Mr. Dunatto stops talking to the guard by the exit door. "Oh, my God...I have got to hear this."

Mrs. Fontanella steps away from her husband. "Your Honor, judge. I can see now that this whole thing was a big mistake. Yes, I did want my mother in the nursing home, but it was at the insistence of my husband."

Mrs. Fontanella's husband stands up. "Lorileigh!"

Mrs. Fontanella ignores her husband and continues, "My husband didn't want her around even though she helped bring up our children and cooked and cleaned and helped out way beyond what she really had to. We have a cleaning lady you see..."

The judge interrupts, "Yes, Mrs. Fontanella, we understand. Please continue with the more pertinent facts."

"Sorry, Your Honor. Anyway, he heard what happened between me and Mrs. Avero and he was mad. It was his and Art Dunnato's idea to try to sue the nursing home. They would have to settle and accept my mother, but I didn't want to do it. They said they would do it with or without me."

Mrs. Fontanella looks over at her mother and a couple of tears run down Mrs. Fontanella's cheek. "I can see now it was such a mistake. My mother looks so happy and I want her to forgive me. I don't want any part of this and if they continue, I will be a witness for the defense stating that they forced me into it."

At that point, people applaud. The judge tries not to show her delight in what Mrs. Fontanella is saying. She bangs the gavel, and the courtroom settles down.

"In that case, let me help you Mrs. Fontanella; this case is dismissed."

Again, the courtroom breaks out in applause and cheers.

"Wait, Your Honor. There is something else."

"Mrs. Fontanella, what else could there possibly be?"

"I want a divorce and I want my husband out of my house."

Mr. Fontanella sits with his mouth open. Again, the courtroom breaks out in cheers and again the judge brings down her gavel.

"Mrs. Fontanella, that is all well and good but that is for a lawyer to address. Perhaps Mr. Russo can direct you unless it becomes a conflict of interest. In any event, this case is dismissed and court is adjourned."

The judge gets up and walks over to the bailiff, who is trying not to laugh. Mr. Russo walks over to Mrs. Fontanella and hands her his card.

"Here. Mrs. Fontanella. Make an appointment and we'll see."

Mrs. Fontanella takes the card and looks at Mr. Russo. "Oh...Ok."

They laugh, and then Mrs. Fontanella reaches out and shakes Mr. Russo's hand.

"Thank you. I want to apologize, especially to you, Mrs. Avero. Thank God you didn't listen to me. Excuse me, I have to see my mother."

Mr. Russo turns to Mrs. Avero and her father-in-law. "This is worse than a cheesy Perry Mason episode."

Mrs. Avero, who is trying not to laugh, chimes in. "No! Much worse. Who would even believe this?!"

They all laugh.

Mr. Russo puts his papers in his briefcase, latches it, and puts his hand on Mrs. Avero's shoulder. "By the way, how did you know where Mrs. Vuolo was?"

"Easy. I had her cousin's address from a card that Mrs. Vuolo had sent me to thank me for standing up for her. I had the return address and asked some of the nosy neighbors."

Again, they all laugh. Mr. San Giorgio and his sons come over and hug Mrs. Avero and she introduces them to her father-in-law. Then Mrs. Avero's father-in-law looks at the people leaving the courtroom and whispers to Mrs. Avero, "Who are those other people? Do they work at the nursing home?"

Mrs. Avero kisses her father-in-law on the cheek and whispers in his ear. "The whole kitchen staff. I needed bodies here!"

"Anna. I know you told me this before, but how did you get in contact with your father?"

"After Enzo Buonoforte died, his daughter was looking for a place for her mother, Enzo's wife. I didn't realize it at the time, but there was a close family connection that had been lost. Mrs. Fonte, the daughter, gave me information about my birth and situation and I looked the family up."

"And now your mother is going to marry him after all these years?"

"It is interesting how someone's death can affect people they didn't even know. Amazing."

Chapter 23
The Basilica of Santa Maria in Trastevere, Rome, February 2, 1963

"Ladies and gentlemen, the captain has put on the fasten seat belt sign. So please buckle your seat belt. We are preparing for our final descent into Rome Airport. Please put away your tray tables, put your seatback up, and put out any cigarettes. And again, thank you for flying, Alitalia." The stewardess makes the same announcement in Italian.

Bruno Sessino put his seatback up and looked around the cabin. He thought again how lucky he was that his niece worked for Alitalia and was able to get him into first class. He was thankful for only taking his carry-on bag.

He remembers the conversation he had with Don Carlo a few days ago at Enzo's wake. "Bruno. I want you to go to Rome and see if you can determine if the Crucifix is authentic or a fake," Don Carlo said. He handed Bruno a folder. "When you read these papers, they will direct you where to go and what to do. Don't let these papers out of your sight."

Bruno looked puzzled. "Why now, after all this time?"

Don Carlo looked away and then at Bruno. "Chiara and her husband want to know what to do with the Crucifix." Don Carlo looked away again.

"Don Carlo, my dear friend. What is wrong?"

"Just old age, dear friend, and just moving on. I can't live forever and I have been having more dreams about my Angelina and Beatrice. I guess my welcoming committee…if I'm fortunate to make it to heaven because I am sure that is where they are."

Both men laughed.

"Don Carlo, you have years to go."

"Even so Bruno. I want this thing with the Crucifix cleared up. Chiara and her family have it now and it is only fair we don't leave them with a mess. Again, the paperwork and where it will direct you will help us finally figure out the authenticity of the Crucifix. If we're lucky, it will turn out to be a fake and not a priceless Michelangelo sculpture. Otherwise…"

As Bruno put the attaché case on his lap, the stewardess walked past him to the back of the first-class section to talk to a tall man who was walking through the curtain separating first class from the rest of the plane.

"Excuse me, sir. We have not been cleared to taxi into our gate."

She waited a moment to make sure the man spoke English and was prepared to ask him the same question in Italian just as he answered her.

"Excuse me. I want to use the lavatory but they are all full and I have an urgent need…" then he smiled and whispered, "…if you know what I mean."

Coach passengers are not allowed in first class, but the stewardess understood the man's need, so she nodded and they walked to the lavatory. As the man passed Bruno's seat, he knocked Bruno's elbow and some papers he was reading fell to the floor. The man bent down and picked up the papers, one of which was a picture of a Crucifix under glass. He looked at it for a few seconds, smiled, and handed it to Bruno.

"Mi scusi signore."

This sent a chill down Bruno's spine. He didn't know why, but it did. As the man came back from the lavatory, he walked by Bruno, looking ahead, and didn't glance at Bruno. This bothered Bruno more than if the man had smiled as he walked by. Bruno dismissed the incident and went over his plans in his head. He was going to get off the plane, take the train from the airport into Rome, and then take a taxi to one of the oldest churches in Rome: The Basilica of Santa Maria in Piazza di Santa Maria in Trastevere. It is there where supposedly a painting was hanging on one wall of the basilica of the warrior pope, Pope Julius II, and next to him on a side table was the Crucifix. Bruno would compare the picture of the Crucifix next to the painting of Pope Julius II to determine the best he can if the picture matches the painting. He would check into the Holiday Inn near the airport and leave the next day for home. A simple plan. He felt it was a shame he couldn't stay longer in Rome, but his instructions were to get back to the United States the next day, not taking any chance that something might go wrong. In the past, art experts and Vatican historians sent letters to the Vatican Museum, wanting to know the location of the painting of Julius II and why it was moved out of the Vatican Museum. The Vatican wanted to know why this sudden interest.

Bruno was very anxious to get off the plane as soon as it landed. He didn't even want to look back in coach to see if the tall man was getting up. When Bruno got off the plane, he raced to the train station inside the airport, bought a ticket, boarded the train, and sat down, looking out the window to see if he was followed, scolding himself for being so paranoid.

When the train arrived in Rome, he was more relaxed and got a taxi to the church. It was a slow taxi ride because of the morning work traffic. He looked around and again was regretful he was not able to stay in Rome longer. He hadn't been here since the war when he did some work for the Italian resistance against Mussolini and the Germans and was glad to see Rome had returned to somewhat normal. With movies like Fellini's La Dolce Vita, and movie stars like Sophia Loren, Gino Lollobrigida, and Marcello Mastroianni, Rome was again a romantic destination.

When the taxi arrived at the church, Bruno paid the driver and walked to the church entrance. He stopped to admire the beautiful façade of The Basilica of Santa Maria in Trastevere, with the clock tower and the paintings over the front portico. He looked around to see if he was being followed and again scolded himself for being so paranoid.

As he walked into the church, he placed his attaché case in his left hand, dipped his fingers in holy water, and made the sign of the cross. He looked around. Once again, his paranoia spiked a little. The church was empty except for a few nuns lighting candles at the side altar. He walked to the left of the main altar, where there were small alcoves with side altars dedicated to certain saints. Near the statues of the saints were small offerings of rosary beads, notes, flowers, and candles, probably from families asking for their prayers to be answered, or some being grateful for unanswered prayers.

As he approached the front of the church, he looked to his right and there it was. A huge painting of Pope Julius II; the pope who forced Michelangelo to paint the ceiling of the Sistine Chapel. Michelangelo was supposedly the artist who sculpted the small gold Christ when he was an artist's apprentice, and then he had it put on the cross. Why Pope Julius II has the Crucifix is unknown. It was possibly a gift from Michelangelo after one of the many disagreements he had with the Pope over the ceiling. There was a way to prove Michelangelo was the artist, but the Crucifix would have to be taken apart. If it was authentic and if the information was made public, there would also be a scandal regarding how it left the Vatican Museum and who was in possession of it. Above all, if it could be authenticated, it would be priceless and could be sold in the black art market.

Bruno, now at the front of the church, kneeled at the altar, blessed himself, and slowly moved toward the painting. There it was in the painting to the right side of Pope Julius II on a small table with the Pope's right hand opened and his index finger pointing to the Crucifix. However, it wasn't under a glass dome. To actually have seen it in the life-sized painting of Julius II left Bruno dumbstruck. He looked around and when he was sure no one was watching; he took the small camera from his attaché case and took several pictures at different angles and close-ups. Removing the picture of Enzo's crucifix from his attaché case, he compared it to the painting. He was stunned by a hand gripping his right shoulder so he couldn't turn around.

"Che Bella! It is a beautiful painting, no?"

Bruno turned his head. It wasn't the man on the plane like he thought it would be. Bruno was shocked but not altogether surprised.

"Don't be so surprised, signore. You led us right to it. We've been wondering about the Crucifix for a very long time."

Bruno pulled loose of the man's grip.

"Who are you? What do you want?"

"Let's just say we are very concerned about the whereabouts of the Crucifix and getting our hands on it once again."

"Once again? Are you from the Vatican?" asked Bruno.

The man just laughed, took the picture of Enzo's crucifix from Bruno, and walked up to the painting to compare it. Bruno stepped away from the painting and would leave in a hurry if he must. After a few seconds, the man seemed angry, said some swear words in Italian, and walked backward to Bruno, who was standing there frozen.

After a few more seconds, the man turned around. "Well, well, well. We are both fooled." He gives the picture of Enzo's crucifix back to Bruno. "*Your* Crucifix is a fake, a clever copy. Look, Christ's head is going the opposite way in your picture. Even the color is wrong. Christ is almost black, but in the painting, he is gold. Signore, we both wasted a trip...lucky for you. Ciao."

The man walked away laughing, which echoed in the church and got the attention of the nuns kneeling in the first row, whose prayers were interrupted. Bruno whispered to himself, *What does he mean I am lucky it was a fake?* The comment again sent a chill down his spine. Bruno couldn't believe he came all this way to see that the Crucifix was a fake. Such reliable sources were certain it was real, but a picture of the painting was needed.

Shaking his head, Bruno took a magnifying glass from his attaché case and looked again at the Crucifix in the painting. He shook his head because it looked exactly like the picture, but the man was right. Christ's head was tilted the wrong way. But then Bruno peered more carefully, and he saw Christ's body and the angle of his bent knees were also at a different angle. Why didn't the man mention that?

Bruno moved his magnifying glass down and saw something written on the base of the Crucifix that was hard to see without the magnifying glass. He took out a piece of paper and wrote down the words: Iesvs Nazarenvs Rex Ivdaeorvm. Using the magnifying glass, he tried to see if it was written on the bottom of the Crucifix base in the picture of Enzo's crucifix. He moved to where there was a little better light and was startled.

Dear God! The words in this picture are backward! The picture was printed backward! Was this intentional?! He looked carefully at the painting and then again at the picture. It was the same with the background behind the Crucifix, but it was in reverse! In the picture, the figure of Christ was black, but that could be intentional, or had it just tarnished over time? Yes, the picture was a little grainy, but it couldn't be mistaken. The picture had been developed in reverse.

Again, he wondered if it was intentional. *Was there a chance he would be followed, and the picture was given to him in reverse to protect him? Why wasn't he told if that was the case?* He put the picture and the magnifying glass in his attaché case and looked around for a side door to leave. He saw a door to the right of the altar but instead of walking to the door; he walked over to the nuns.

"Scusi. Do any of you speak English?"

They laughed a little and one nun said, "Sorry! We all do. We're from America for a Vatican Council Meeting."

Bruno showed them the piece of paper on which he had written the words, Iesvs Nazarenvs Rex Ivdaeorvm.

"Sisters, can you tell me what this means?"

The nuns looked at the paper, and then the first nun handed the paper back to Bruno.

"It means, *Jesus of Nazareth, King of the Jews.*"

"Thank you, Sister. I thought it may say that, but I wasn't sure."

"You're very welcome. Where did you see that?"

"Oh. Over there. On the base of the Crucifix in the painting."

"Oh yes. Michelangelo's La Crusifix da Giello di Caprese."

Bruno was shocked. "You mean you know it wasn't sculpted by Michelangelo?"

"I have a doctorate in Renaissance Art and I studied the life of Michelangelo and his work, especially his early work under the artist Domenico Ghirlandaio. Michelangelo studied as Ghirlandaio's apprentice. The sculptor of Christ is mentioned in Ghirlandaio's biographies. The story or myth, whichever, is that when Michelangelo was sixteen, Ghirlandaio helped him get permission from the church to study cadavers. Michelangelo sculpted many small sculptures of Christ as a hobby, using his knowledge of studying the cadavers. It is believed the one in the painting is gold. However, it was never confirmed if Michelangelo melted the gold and made the cast. It might have been Ghirlandaio who really made the cast and sculpted it. The legend is that the true artist's name is somehow inside the base, but since it is missing, we will never know. Anyway, who would break the base, other than a thief? You didn't steal it, did you, signore?"

Bruno and the sister laughed.

"No, Sister. I am just a connoisseur of Italian art and the legend, as it is, is interesting."

Bruno was more excited to hear that Enzo's crucifix could have been sculpted by Michelangelo. Then he thought, *In the painting, Christ is gold. The Crucifix the Buonofortes have has Christ as black. Was it painted black to camouflage it? It's just like the damn Maltese Falcon. This is getting more confusing and maybe scary. I'm out of my depth. I have to get out of here.*

"Thank you, Sister. Very interesting. Thank you."

"You're most welcome."

Bruno stopped on his way out and turned to ask the nuns another question.

"Pardon me, sisters. I have another question. Unlike you, I am a novice studying Michelangelo. I would like to see the Crucifix in person since it is such an interesting and unusual piece of Michelangelo's work."

"Well, if you go to the Vatican Museum, you can see it...a copy, anyway. The original was stolen."

Bruno was surprised at her comment and played dumb. "Stolen when the original was in the Vatican Museum?" he asked.

"The original was lost years ago. No one really knows."

Bruno smiled, thanked the nuns again, and walked on his way. *Could the Vatican have the original and the Buonofortes have a copy,* he thought, *and why the coverup?* He would have to go to the Vatican Museum. But was someone still watching him? He saw an exit door by the small altar to his right and ambled over to it. He pushed the door open, looked around, and then hailed a taxi to take him to the Holiday Inn near the airport.

As Bruno was checking into the hotel, he kept looking around. He asked the attendant if there was room service and was told he could get something to eat in the coffee shop. The attendant would let Bruno know when it opened.

"My brother-in-law runs the coffee shop, and he is coming from the other side of Rome, so sometimes there is traffic. It shouldn't be too long," the attendant said with a small laugh.

Bruno was not paying attention.

"Signore, I will send the maid up with fresh towels. Our washing machine was broken and we're a little behind but I will take care of it 'Subito'."

"Grazie."

Before he left, Bruno asked the desk clerk if he knew when the Vatican Museum was open. The desk clerk took out a notebook where he kept the days and times when the most popular sights and museums were open.

"Ah. Ecco. It is open now until five today, but it is closed tomorrow. If you want to see it now, I can call you a taxi."

Bruno looked at his watch. He had a few hours left before the museum closed. He couldn't wait until the day after tomorrow, since he had the first flight home.

"Yes. Give me about a half hour and I will be right down."

Bruno got his room key and decided to take a shower; too nervous to eat. He wasn't in his room for five minutes when there was a knock at the door. He froze for a moment. "I'll be right there. Subito. I'm changing."

He looked out the peephole and saw the maid with the towels. When he opened the door, the maid stepped aside and two men walked into the room and shut the door behind them.

"Buon Giorno, Signor Sessino. Don't be alarmed. I will explain."

One man sat in a chair and motioned to Bruno to sit as well. Meanwhile, the other man looked in the bathroom and stood by the window, as if he was keeping watch.

"Signor Sessino. We know who has the Crucifix. More precisely, La Crusifix da Giello di Caprese. The Vatican does not want it back. They want it exactly where it is and do not want it in a church or sold to any dealer or whomever or whatever."

Bruno looked shocked. "I don't understand?"

"Simply put, there are those in prominent positions who believe that the Crucifix is...how can I put it otherwise...they believe it is cursed."

"I still don't understand. How can the church believe it is cursed?"

"I don't know the right word in English, but that is what they believe. You see, they know the history of the Crucifix. There are gaps, but they know the basics."

Bruno got suspicious. "Who are you? How do I know you won't hold me for ransom to get the cross or just steal it?"

The man reached into his jacket pocket, allowing Bruno to see his gun. He produced a wallet and showed Bruno his badge and identification card. Bruno took it and read it.

"Signor Sessino, Mi dispiace. I am sorry. My name is Angelo Arnone. I am the Chief of Special Operations. We do work for the Vatican when they want to keep things quiet and from the public. You know, they don't want the publicity with some things."

"I still don't understand."

"There are people who know what the cross is and they want it. It was seen, and suddenly there is interest again. It was thought to be lost. Now that it has surfaced, it is priceless and there are collectors who would pay. No one can tell at this point. They may even kill for it."

At the mention of possible death, all the blood drained from Bruno's face.

"Scusi, signore. You don't have the cross, so you have nothing to worry about right now. Let me ask you, when you were in the church, who did you see?"

"I saw some nuns."

"Are you *sure* they were nuns?"

"Well, I asked them a question about the writing above the Crucifix and they knew."

"Signor, a thief would know everything about the Crucifix. And, as far as we know, you are right, they are nuns. But we don't know about anyone else in the church."

Bruno doesn't know whether to mention anything about the man who approached him. Then he thought it best to mention it.

"There was a man who also looked at the painting and my picture of the cross and told me it was a fake."

"That is good. That was the intention of having the picture reversed. If that man took a closer look, he would see the writing on the base of the Crucifix was backward. You were lucky."

"I still don't understand about the curse and..."

"Signor, I have someone downstairs who will explain everything. Then we are going to take you somewhere safe and get you on a plane first thing in the morning. I assume the papers you have are only copies?"

"Yes."

"Please give them to me. The whole file."

Bruno reluctantly handed over the file to the detective.

"Paolo, bring me that wastebasket."

The detective picked a lighter out of his pocket and lit the file in the wastebasket. He placed it near an open window.

"Paolo, when it burns out, take the ashes, put them down the toilet, and clean the wastebasket."

"Ecco. Let me call downstairs and have our Vatican historian explain everything to you. Then we go to dinner and get you to a safe place to sleep."

The detective called, and in a few minutes, there was a knock at the door. The detective opened the door, and a person walked in.

"Buon Giorno."

Bruno was dumbstruck. "You're kidding me!"

Chapter 24
St. Mary's Hospital February 3, 1963

The phone rang in Marti Bonantti's hospital room. He had been rushed into emergency surgery because the swelling of his brain wasn't going down after the accident and the pressure had to be relieved. His wife and two children were allowed to wait in his room since it was a private room in a private wing of the hospital, paid for by Mr. Genovesse. Marti's wife Maggie stared out the window. Marti's son decided to sit outside the operating room area to wait for his father to get out of surgery. The phone rang and startled Maggie, but she ignored it. Finally, Marti's daughter Katie answered the phone.

"Hello. Oh, hi Uncle Joey." She looked at her mother who rolled her eyes. "Yeah, we're doing OK. Here, speak to Mom."

Katie was aware of everything that had gone on and she had no desire to talk to her uncle. After a while, there was no way to shield the kids. Too much had gone on. She also was angry at the way her cousins treated her and her brother. Maggie motioned she didn't want to talk to Joey, but Katie stomped her foot and insisted. Finally, Maggie took the receiver.

"Yeah, Joey. What do you want?"

Joey was taken aback by the abrupt way Maggie spoke to him. Everyone was fond of Maggie but this was a side of her they had not seen, except when Joey and Vic met with her a couple of days ago at the hospital.

Maggie gave them some credit for having the balls to come see their brother and face her; and now a phone call. She heard the nervousness in Joey's voice.

"I called to see how Marti is."

She turned and looked out the window. "Well, right now he's being operated on to relieve the pressure on his brain because the swelling has not gone down." There was silence for a few seconds.

"Maggie, Vic is here and we want you to know that if there is anything we can do…"

Maggie instantly shot back. "Are you fucking kidding me! After all the bullshit that you guys pulled! The jealousy and resentment you all showed not only to my husband but to me and my kids. And Vic and his bitch wife! If I saw her again, I would spit in her face!"

Joey tried to interrupt. "Maggie, I don't know what to say."

"I told you guys that if Marti wants to see you that is up to him, but I don't trust any of you because when this thing is over, it will be the same bullshit and we have better things and better people to spend our time with."

Suddenly her son ran into the room all flustered. "Ma, Ma…"

She tried to hang up the phone but the receiver dropped, hitting the floor. Katie shot up from her chair. They were frozen, not knowing what was going on. Was Marti alright? They were afraid to ask and were paralyzed. Was he alive or dead? They could hear Joey on the phone yelling for Maggie. Time stood still.

Chapter 25
St. Mary's Hospital February 4, 1963

Father Ludovico heard the phone ring in the rectory's office. His nights had been mostly sleepless, worrying about Father Tommaso, and performing two funerals days before, as well as his other church and school activities. He put a pillow over his head and hoped the housekeeper, Mrs. Fitzgibbons would hear the phone, otherwise he would have to get up. It wasn't really unusual for the phone to ring at all hours. No one dies conveniently. The phone stopped ringing and he knew in a few minutes, Mrs. Fitzgibbons would scurry up the stairs and knock on his door.

Mrs. Fitzgibbons had been a fixture at Sacred Heart Church ever since her husband was killed accidentally at one of the mills in Botany Village, leaving her with two young sons and a daughter. She had first volunteered at the church and the school before her husband died, so her hard work and dedication were well known. Although she received a large insurance settlement from her husband's company, she wanted to work to occupy her time when her children were in school.

When the old church and rectory housekeeper retired, the pastor immediately hired Mrs. Fitzgibbons. Not everyone was happy to have this feisty little Irish woman in charge. She could have come out of central casting from MGM or one of the other movie studios because she fit the role perfectly of the tough housekeeper, who kept everyone in line and hid her heart of gold.

With the small salary from the church and the investment of her insurance settlement, she could send her two sons to Montclair College. Although at the time a teacher's college, her oldest son became a lawyer and her youngest son an engineer. Her daughter attended Katherine Gibbs Secretarial School, also in Montclair, but worked her way up to a legal assistant at her brother's law firm, where she met her husband.

Mrs. Fitzgibbon's sons married Italian girls and her daughter married an Italian, too. When her oldest son told her he was in love with an Italian, she said she would have preferred he marry an Irish girl. Being surrounded by warm-hearted but tough Italian women, she knew they were the right ones to keep her sons in line. She quickly realized all three had made the right choice.

Her daughter was the last to get married, and afterward, she sold her house on Randolph Avenue and moved into the rectory, with the agreement she could entertain her family whenever she wanted to.

When Father Ludovico first came to Sacred Heart Church, she was so taken with him she shied away not to reveal her feelings. His appearance, charm, and warmth could melt anyone's heart. At first, he saw her as cold and bossy. After a time, she treated him like a surrogate son and was extremely protective.

One time, Father Ludovico overheard her scold someone on the phone who was insisting on something that he couldn't make out. As she was going through Father Ludovico's schedule, she became irate and yelled at the person who seemed to be attacking Father Ludovico and the priesthood.

"I told you his schedule is full that day and don't you dare say he is off playing golf. You watch too many movies! What do you think he does all day? Say a Mass and then go on his way? He has most of the responsibility for the Church and the school. On the weekends he says Masses from 7:00 in the morning till the afternoon. Then, there are the Sunday Masses, and the marriages, *and* the baptisms. He gets calls to do last rites at any time of the day and night. He helps any other parishes in the Diocese that need help. If he is lucky, he takes some well-deserved time off during the summer when he reads and studies, mostly the Scriptures."

She began writing a message and continued talking. "I will give him the message, but don't give him any complaints or you'll have to deal with me. I take all his calls." Then she slammed down the phone. She took the message, crumbled it up, and threw it in the wastepaper basket. "Stupid man."

Father Ludovico had quickly walked away, trying to muffle his laughter.

As Father Ludovico realized the late-night phone call must be important, he heard Mrs. Fitzgibbons, footsteps faster than the usual scurry, coming down the hall. He jumped out of bed, threw on his robe, and looked at the time on the clock radio on the nightstand. *My God, 3:15. Just when I was falling asleep; now what? I hope it's not what I think.*

Instead of the usual mechanical knock on the door, this time he heard a frantic knock that scared him. He tied his robe and opened the door.

"Father, I'm sorry, but it's the hospital." She knew what it was probably about, but she didn't want to tell him. Father Ludovico already knew anyway.

"Alright, Mrs. Fitzgibbons. Let me get my slippers on and I'll be right down."

He put on his slippers and raced to the rectory office with Mrs. Fitzgibbons hustling behind. He lunged for the phone.

"Yes, this is Father Ludovico." The person on the other end was at first stuttering.

"Oh, oh, Father, oh Father. I am sorry to disturb you. This is Sister Sarah. Father Tommaso has taken a turn for the worse. The doctors are with him. He had a coughing fit, and they said he had a heart attack. It seems to be serious because he is calling for you."

This is what Father Ludovico was afraid of. "Okay, Sister. I will be right there." He hung up the phone without waiting for a response. Mrs. Fitzgibbons had already guessed what was happening.

"Father, can I make you a quick cup of coffee you can take with you, and maybe some biscuits?"

He gave her a quick hug. "No, thank you."

He sprinted to his room and changed as quickly as he could. Looking around the room for his coat, he saw the envelope from the London lawyer. He didn't know why, but he grabbed it, stuck it into his inside coat pocket, and left.

There was no traffic, and he got to the hospital in neighboring Passaic in record time. He parked in the front, put the Chaplin's plaque on the dashboard, and ran inside. Stopping at the desk, he explained the situation and didn't wait for questions or a response. He took the elevator to the ICU unit where Sister Sarah met him.

"Hi, Father. I sent the other sisters home. We have been taking shifts."

Then the doctor and a nurse came out of the ICU room. Any introductions at this point weren't necessary.

"Doctor, what is happening?" Father Ludovico asked.

The doctor dismissed the nurse and took Father Ludovico aside. "Oh, Father. It is good you are here. He had a coughing fit that caused a heart attack. After all the testing, it appears this was not the only attack he had. He probably ignored the others. His lungs and arteries aren't in the greatest shape because of the smoking. He's a tough one, though. We will keep him comfortable and see if he can recover."

Father Ludovico was half listening. He was looking past the doctor, trying to fight back tears, seeing Father Tommaso in an oxygen tent. "Okay, doctor. Let me go into him now."

"Oh, Father. He was calling for a *Gianni*. Is that you?" the doctor asked.

Father Ludovico wiped tears from his eyes and just nodded. He walked in, sat in a chair by the bed, and held Father Tommaso's hand. Tommaso's breathing was very shallow. A nurse who was sitting in the corner walked over and whispered to Father Ludovico that if he needed anything to just ask. He nodded and smiled weakly. He stood and bent over the oxygen tent and gently shook Father Tommaso's arm.

"Tommaso. Hey, you old goat. What are you doing? We have a vacation to plan." Father Ludovico knew there might be no vacation, but what else could he say?

Father Tommaso slowly opened his eyes and tried to speak. "Oh, Gianni. I heard you, but I thought it was a dream. My dear friend and brother. We're going to take that vacation, as God is my witness. He isn't ready for me yet. But if He is calling, I want you to know..." He took another breath to speak. "I want you to know Gianni, there is no other man I love more than you. You are a better man and a better priest than I could have ever been. Your inspiration saved me many times from making foolish mistakes."

Father Ludovico was now crying openly. He had not felt such pain, such anguish, since holding Sister Bernadette as she died. He tried to compose himself. "Tommaso, *you* were *my* inspiration and..." To compose himself, Father Ludovico took a mental inventory of the items he had brought to conduct Father Tommaso's last rites. He had what he needed. Then he remembered the envelope in his inside pocket. He struggled to decide what to do with the papers and then Father Tommaso tried to raise himself.

He looked at Father Ludovico and smiled and squeezed his hand. Father Ludovico took the envelope with the legal papers. "Tommaso, a lawyer from London, traveled to give you these papers. I have them for you and..."

Father Tommaso's voice was a little strained and Father Ludovico stood over the oxygen tent and pulled it down a bit to hear him. Father Tommaso tried to raise himself up. "Gianni, you are my sole heir. If anything happens, as a last wish, please take care of things. Sister Sarah has my will and other papers...I am sorry...please understand..."

Father Ludovico crushed the papers in his hand when he saw Father Tommaso lay back down. Still smiling, Father Tommaso closed his eyes and his head gently lay on the pillow toward Father Ludovico.

"Nurse!" Father Ludovico yelled.

The nurse ran over and took Father Tommaso's pulse. "He's ok, Father. The doctor gave him something to help him sleep. It's best that he rests. He's a tough one, God bless him."

Father Ludovico sat back down and held Father Tommaso's hand. Then he looked at the papers in his hand and shoved them back into his inside jacket pocket. The nurse walked around the bed and adjusted Father Tommaso's blankets.

"Father, if there is anything you need, I will stay here until another nurse relieves me."

Father Ludovico gave her a half-hearted smile and like a small child asked, "Nurse, do you think he will be ok?"

She came around the bed to Father Ludovico, smiled, and whispered. "Well, Father, you people are in charge of the miracles." The nurse gently touched Father Ludovico's shoulder and went back to her seat in the corner.

Father Ludovico looked at Father Tommaso. "You're damn right we are."

About the Author

Dr. Frank Plateroti earned his Doctorate Degree in Education Research and a Master's Degree in Communication, with a concentration in psychology. For the past twenty years, Dr. Plateroti has taught in the communication department at William Paterson University in New Jersey. Some of the courses he has taught are television production, media studies, and his specialty; intrapersonal and interpersonal communication.

Prior to his teaching, he worked in public relations and was a television producer, writer, and director working with network and cable news companies and formed his own international production company. Today, Dr. Plateroti has further established his writing career by republishing the 2024 updated and expanded first book of his trilogy, East Clifton Avenue, Origins, Second Edition, which he has self-published under Plateroti Communications. Book Two of the series, The Next Generation, will be released at the same time as Book One. East Clifton Avenue, Books One and Two, are available on Amazon and other online book websites.

He has also published Speak No Evil, In Search of Our Self-Esteem, Self-Identity, and Self-worth, and is currently writing a second edition which will be available in early fall, 2024, on Amazon and other online book websites. Speak No Evil is the culmination of twenty years of teaching the university communications course he developed. Dr. Plateroti describes his teaching experience as "the most rewarding period of my total adult career."

Dr. Plateroti is active in award-winning home renovations, maintaining his real estate and financial investments, and is also a recording vocalist.